THE LAST CRYSTAL
ARROW

AF295172

Ravi Sharma

BlueRoseONE.com
Stories Matter

First Published in May 2022

ISBN: 978-93-5611-188-2

BLUEROSE PUBLISHERS

www.bluerosepublishers.com

info@bluerosepublishers.com

+91 8882 898 898

Cover Design:

Aveek

Typographic Design:

Pooja Sharma

Email

ravi.connectme@gmail.com

Distributed by: BlueRose, Amazon, Flipkart

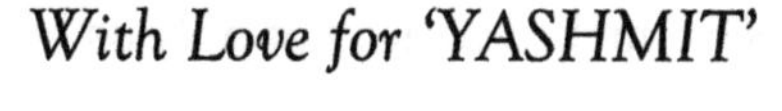

With Love for 'YASHMIT'

<u>**Making a 'Right Choice' Matters**</u>

It is very important to choose the right option

The decisions we make impact not only us but also all the people around us.

Be wise, critical, sensible, and responsible.

-   Ravi Sharma

Contents

Chapter 1: The Beginning

There was noise everywhere, soldiers were running for their lives. There were dead bodies scattered around, someone's brother, someone's son, and someone's friend!

Somebody was running away with his severed hand, while someone's leg had been chopped off. They just wanted to hide somewhere so that somehow their life could be saved. There was an orgy of death all over the battlefield.

Who would have thought that Thanjavur would ever see this day? Despite being a mighty kingdom and having a mighty king, today it was nearing its end.

There was a hideous scene all around, everyone was begging for mercy.

Mercy? Markooz's army had never heard the word, nor had it been taught to them. They were just taught cruelty. They went on destroying. His army of demons started eating the soldiers alive and did not leave even bones.

Thanjavur's army was not weak, but they have lost their confidence. Perhaps they had never seen such a cruel and cannibal army. There was only death everywhere, heaps of dead bodies, soldiers wailing in pain and running away after saving their lives.

But some warriors were not scared, not tired, and were fighting relentlessly. Their king was still alive, and they knew that their victory is certain as long as he is alive.

Even the enemy knew very well that it is impossible to conquer Thanjavur as long as Nirvana is alive.

Haliba, the commander of Markooz, was aware of this. No matter how much destruction they had caused to Thanjavur, none of his warriors and demons could even reach Nirvana, so killing him was a far cry.

Nirvana, eight feet tall, muscular, wide chested, strong, cunning, agile, and brave king was on the battlefield to save his country and people. With the long and heavy sword held by his strong hands, he was destroying the enemies. More than ten days have passed, and now only a handful of people were left in his army. Even then he was not scared, tired, or defeated, just kept on killing.

Seeing his valor and bravery, now the courage of Markooz's army was started to break down and his soldiers also started fleeing. The entire army of demons was destroyed, and he was inflicting a deadly blow on the remaining army. It seemed that Nirvana alone would destroy everyone. They were all frightened, and the steps of Haliba also started retreating and he started running away leaving the battlefield.

Nirvana convinced his warriors to attack the soldiers while running away. And soon the enemy forces fled from the battlefield. Nirvana was standing alone with some of his soldiers. There was a scene of destruction around the battlefield, with burning chariots, weapons, and heaps of corpses.

The soldiers of Thanjavur started celebrating victory and started dancing with joy.

Their eyes went to his king Nirvana, they saw their king riding in his chariot, heavy and strong iron shields on his back, a bow on his shoulders, and a chariot full of sharp and long arrows. With one hand he held the reins of both the horses tied to the chariot and in the other hand a heavy and long sword. He was standing in the middle of the battlefield.

Shocked they looked at each other and ran to their king.

"The fight is over my lord", a soldier said, "it's time to go back home and pay homage to our brave soldier who fought till death for the pride of our kingdom".

Nirvana looked at each of them with teary eyes and smiled.

"It's not over until either me or Markooz is alive. The final fight is yet to begin. I urge you all to go back to the city and ask everyone to immediately go to a safer place. I give you all the responsibility of saving the lives of everyone", said Nirvana. "Leave immediately, I don't want anyone on the battlefield. Treat this as my last command if I don't come back alive", Nirvana said.

"Have you not heard me Parkus?", Nirvana asked his charioteer.

"Sorry sir, but a charioteer cannot leave his king alone on the battlefield. You will need me, and I want to fight this last war with you, 'if this is the last war'", Parkus replied.

"Can I ask you a question? You are a great, extremely brave, and mighty king. I can't even see the fear in your eyes, why have you asked everyone to move to a safe place? I am sure,

Markooz will not be able to stand before you and will be killed, so why are you calling this your last war. Why did my king send his army to obey his last command? Why does he want to fight alone and is asking his charioteer to go too?" Parks asked.

"We should make choices according to the situation, and I want to ensure the safety of my people in my life", Nirvana replied. "As long as I stand here, neither Markooz nor any of his warriors can enter my kingdom and harm anyone. But I very well know his plight and cruelty. I am neither weak nor afraid and will fight with him till my last breath. He is not a brave warrior, but a deceiver and an elusive. I am ready to fight with him, but I have no solution for his army of dead souls and black magic. But I will fight till my family and my people are safe. Because if he and his army enter the city, they will give everyone a heart-wrenching painful death. So, I have ordered everyone to go to a safe place".

"We don't have time Parkus. Follow my orders, save your family, yourself, and as many people as you can", Nirvana said.

Parkus looked at the brave eyes of his king, bowed down to him, and started moving towards the city. While walking, he looked back and asked, "What message should this charioteer give to his queen from your side, my lord?"

Nirvana said, "A queen has the same duty as a king. Ask your queen to protect her country and her people. But yes, please convey a husband's message to his wife. Tell her that I am sorry to leave her alone in this tough situation, and please ask her to take care of herself, my son, and my family".

Parkus walked on with moist eyes, he did not look back.

Now Nirvana was ready for the decisive battle. His heavy shield was now light because he knew that his people were safe. The grip of his sword was strengthened, as he had taken a vow to behead every enemy.

A whirlwind of dust covered the sky, the rumble of horses reverberating everywhere. Horror spirits started roaming around Nirvana. It was the deadly and elusive army of Markooz whose job was to suck every drop of blood from the enemy's body.

A large number of warriors and an army of demons were also moving forward to attack him.

Nirvana did not panic. He proceeded to roar and went on destroying the enemy. Once again, he was not under anyone's control. He freed the chariots and horses from the warriors. A brave king was fighting for his kingdom, the safety, and the life of his people. It was not possible to stop him.

Markooz's army had begun to flee the battlefield once again. He fired innumerable arrows from his bow and kept on destroying his army. But he could not control the spirits. They were frightening him, hitting his body with sharp objects. His body was bleeding, but even then, he kept fighting. Rarely had anyone seen a warrior fighting alone with thousands of soldiers. There was someone who was watching his bravery and would narrate his heroic saga to the whole world.

Now perhaps the end of the war was near. The earth was shaking as if an earthquake was coming. With the rumble of horses, Markooz entered the battlefield.

Markooz was a cruel, ruthless, and cunning warrior. Scary face, long thick hair, big red eyes, which make the soul tremble at the sight. Now he had come to the battlefield. This was a strange and rare sight as he was riding on his four-headed horse. Surely no one had ever seen such a horse.

His big red eyes were searching for his enemy Nirvana.

Nirvana was brutally killing his soldiers. Seeing this, Markooz's anger had reached its peak. He challenged him to battle in his terrible and heavy voice and ran towards him.

It was by no means less than Clash of Titans. Both the warriors attacked each other with all their might. The whole sky reverberated with the clash of the two spears. Their weapons were colliding with terrific light and energy as if many volcanoes had erupted. It seemed like a never-ending war. Both the warriors were inflicting deadly blows on each other, but Markooz could not bear the deadly blow of Nirvana for long.

Markooz was fighting, but he was now scared. None of his weapons could stop Nirvana. The victory of truth over lies was certain. He understood that it is not easy to defeat and kill him.

Now he had only one option, deceit. He invoked his black magic and spirits and shot an arrow toward Nirvana. It was an infallible power, for which Nirvana had no solution. The arrow went out penetrating his body. He was badly injured, and blood started flowing from all over his body. Seeing him injured, the soldiers of Markooz started attacking him. Nirvana kept on fighting, inflicting fatal blows, and eventually, he fell to the ground.

Crossing all limits, he also drank the blood from Nirvana's chest and laughed loudly saying, "Today my and my mother's revenge is complete."

It was a very painful scene. The end of a great warrior was near. His eyes were wide open as if he is watching the ruin of his kingdom.

Markooz moved forward. When someone grabbed his leg, he looked back, and his senses were blown away. Nirvana held onto Mark's leg tightly with one hand. Despite being injured, he was fighting till his last breath. He cut off Nirvana's hand with the sharp strike of his ax and moved on.

He ordered Haliba and his soldiers to move toward the city.

"Don't leave anyone, be a small child, old or a woman, kill everyone. No one should survive to take revenge, and no one should be alive to tell what happened here. No mercy, just destroy everyone", he ordered and left.

"Let no one escape", Haliba ordered.

Haliba and his soldiers crossed all limits of cruelty. Children were buried alive. The girls and women were rapped before their families and killed.

Like cannibals, they lashed out at the people. Some ate people alive, and many were beheaded.

Haliba stepped forward and attacked the palace. Its doors were closed. After much effort, the door broke. His eyes were looking for Nirvana's wife and son. Then he heard some sounds from one of the royal rooms. Thinking the royal family hiding there, he ordered the soldiers to put the room on fire.

Soldiers soaked every door, window, the wall with oil and set them on fire. The children and women inside the room began to scream and cry. Their cry was pleasing to Haliba's ears which he thoroughly enjoyed. The whole city had now turned into a crematorium, and he was convinced that no one was left.

Ensuring no one was alive, they raised their victory flag on Thanjavur.

"Everyone has been killed, my king. It's all over", said Haliba

Markooz turned to Haliba and asked, "Nirvana's family?"

"Burned alive", he replied with a smile.

"Praise the return of the warriors now, they must be tired. Offer good food and wine to them also", Markooz left, congratulating Haliba.

It was night and dark, with staggering steps someone entered the battlefield. Her moist eyes were searching for Nirvana.

She called out to him with a heavy voice. She was Durgashakti, the wife of Nirvana.

Nirvana was still alive, perhaps he was waiting for her.

He called out, "I am here my queen".

Durgashakti came running to him and started crying bitterly.

With trembling hands, she held Nirvana's head in her lap and lovingly caressed his forehead.

"I am proud of you my king", said while hugging him.

"I was only waiting for you my love, wanted to see you for the last time before I leave", Nirvana replied.

They kept looking at each other, holding and talking in silence.

The tears flowing from Durgashakti's eyes were rolling all over his face. Now his pain had subsided, and he took his last breath.

He left her forever and she kept crying grabbing him in her arms.

A voice approached her ears saying, "The danger is not averted yet, my queen. We must go".

She nodded, took off a robe over Nirvana's corpse, and bowed with folded hands. There were no more tears in her eyes, there was no trembling in her voice. She gathered all her courage, kept the severed hand of Nirvana near his body, and cremated him with her own hands.

She collected all the scriptures of Nirvana and placed them on his chariot.

"Now we must go", she said, got on the chariot, and left.

Deep in her heart, she promised herself to fulfill the last wish of her king.

As she left the battlefield, her confidence grew stronger. She took all the survivors along and left.

Chapter 2: The Rejuvenate

15 Years Later

"I knew you can't go without meeting me, without seeing me", Durgashakti said while putting her hand on his forehead.

"How could I go on without meeting you, my queen, my love, my life? These few breaths were waiting for you only".

Tears falling from Durgashakti's eyes were falling on Nirvana's forehead and narrating her pain.

"I am fine, my king, your every wish will be obeyed. I will ensure the safety of all the people. I will teach all of them to live again and try to provide a good life for all of them", she said sobbing.

"You must support all of them. All the duties of a queen have to be performed to the fullest. Our son will have to become a brave warrior and rebuild this scattered kingdom", Nirvana extended his blood-soaked hand and said, "Promise me!"

She kissed his forehead and replied, "I promise!"

"But how will I do all this without you", she asked but he had left, his eyes were wide open.

Durgashakti got up in a panic.

"You have been gone for years, but it feels as if yesterday

You are never parted, your fragrance, your touch is with me every moment

Life has returned everything today, maybe I am happy too. But you will always be missed."

- Durgashakti

After the death of Nirvana, she brought all the people to the safe island of Phalsa.

Phalsa was a lonely island in the middle of the deep sea, which no one had reached yet. Durgashakti heard from her father many times that there is an island by this name many miles away in the south direction, but it had just seemed to be a story.

They needed a similar place to hide from Markooz and his army. They had reached after long and difficult traveling many days and nights hungry and thirsty.

15 years had passed and for Queen Dugshakti it was as if yesterday.

The scene on the battlefield, the people screaming in pain, the corpse, and the death of Nirvana in her arms were unforgettable.

Durgashakti had made Phalsa a self-sufficient island, which was a brilliant display of her leadership and enterprising skills. Everything needed for a good life was made available there. They started a fresh and new beginning including their identity. She was now known as "Chandrika". They not only changed their names but also their way of dressing.

Now Phalsa had become famous. Weapons made from the bones of animals and whales made here were quite popular. People from far away kingdoms used to come to buy them.

Not only the weapons but also the coconuts, dry fruits, and ships were in the trade all over, and eventually, it became a flourishing island.

Nirvana's son Samuel was now a 22-year-old young hunk. He was as strong as his father and very active and quick.

In the blink of an eye, he could climb huge mountains. Running with tigers and chasing foxes in the woods was his most loved hobby. Hardly anyone had ever seen a boy riding huge whale fish in the forest, but he was an expert in that. Everyone was very impressed by his power and fascinated by his speed, except for his mother.

One afternoon, he heard someone calling him.

"Samuel, Samuel!"

"Yes, say what happened, why are you shouting out your lungs, Prithvi?", he said

"Your search is on, come on soon, the clan chief 'Chandrika' has called you. I mean your mother", Prithvi gasped.

"Hmm, let's go but what do you mean "my search is on"?", Samuel asked

"Oho, I mean we were searching for you for a long. Many soldiers have been sent to the woods to find you but luckily, I got you. Come on, move fast now", Prithvi replied while walking quickly.

Soon they both reached.

"Here is you son chief. I should be awarded a delicious meal now, it was so hard to find him", Prithvi said curiously.

Chandrika said with a smile, "Of course. But you eat a little less, I am afraid someday you may finish all the food on this island". And they both started laughing out loud.

Chandrika looked at Samuel in anger and asked strictly, "Where were you?"

"I was just walking around in the woods", Samuel replied.

"When will you grow up? You go missing all day! Do you have any sense of your responsibility or not?", she chided. "You are now 22 years old and certainly not a kid. There are many boys of your age here who help in the work of the clan, and some keep learning some skill or art almost every day. Samuel, you have the responsibility for this island and your people, and you must understand this now."

Samuel stood with his head bowed and listened.

"However, we have to go somewhere tomorrow, to prepare the ship. Keep 10 days' food and everything you need. We will leave tomorrow morning. Now go and rest because this journey will be long", Chandrika said.

"May I know where we are going Mom?", asked Samuel.

"Every person has a goal in life that needs a journey, and this is the beginning of yours. You would know your answers, probably you already know. Wait for the correct time, you may leave now and take some good rest", she said.

Samuel went to his room.

"It's not okay to be so harsh with him. And what is the need for him to push towards a goal he doesn't need to achieve now? You must forget the past Durgashakti. A new beginning has already started. You have a great island with you now, your people are happy. You have fulfilled your commitment. Everyone is happy, being here. Please don't push them to the dark again. Together you and Samuel can make this place even better", her father Drupad said.

Durgashakti was standing on the balcony of the palace looking toward the sea.

Without turning back, she said,

"Maybe you're right, he doesn't need it. When we came to the island, we changed our name, identity, clothes, everything but our existence has not changed. From Durgashakti I became Chandrika, do you think I have achieved anything? Father!!! No.... I have only seen losses; loss of self-respect, my dreams, the childhood of my son, and innumerable lives of my people.

She turned towards him, holding his hand,

"Do you see these people around? They all seem calm, busy, smiling, and happy but there is a fierce volcano hidden in their hearts. None of them have any complaints or questions for 'Chandrika' because she gave them a new and safe life. But they certainly have many for 'Durgashakti'. We all had to leave our house, and relatives one night and today are living with an expectation of going back. See their questioning eyes asking every day. Will we be getting justice? Will we ever go back again? Will he ever be punished?"

Tears welled up in her eyes and there was sadness in her voice, she said

"Many fathers among them could not even perform the last rites of their sons. Many mothers have cried on the dead bodies of their sons. There are so many brothers & sisters who have left their families to die and burn. There is also a queen in all of them whose king breathed his last in her lap. And there is also a son who could not even see his father for the last time."

"We had no choice that day except to come here hide overnight and settle down. It was our compulsion, not our destiny. We all have to fight to regain our identity. Our names cannot be included in history as fugitives or among the dead. All those who died that day were martyrs and those who are alive will have to regain their identity and self-respect."

"Nirvana and my promise were not only to save our people and give them a good life. Our promise is also to return Thanjavur to existence. The sacrifice of Nirvana cannot go in vain."

"This struggle is for all of us. It is not personal for me but as the queen, I must perform my duties. And this is the duty of Samuel as well. We are all nothing less than a living corpse, we want our soul back, otherwise very soon we will all die", she replied

The next morning Samuel and Chandrika started their journey.

Crossing the ocean for 3 days, they reached Krishak. It was a small kingdom situated in the north direction at the Flora Hills. This kingdom was not ruled by any king and was known as a center of education for its excellence and brilliance. Students from far and wide used to come here for training and studies. Everyone here was equal whether from a royal family or an ordinary person. The second reason for the fame of this state was its teacher, "Lionel".

Lionel was a very powerful personality who was an expert in all forms of fights, war policy, scripture, and spiritual Magic. Getting admitted & education in his monastery was not easy.

It was evening before the sunset. Samuel and Chandrika reached the monastery.

Lionel was busy with a lamb.

"Greeting's teacher", Chandrika said

"The meeting time is over madam", Lionel replied humbly without even looking at them.

"We are sorry", both replied and left to sit under a tree in front of the monastery.

"Who is he, mother?", Samuel asked.

"He is the anchor of your journey my son, your teacher. I just wish that he agrees to mentor you", she replied.

They sat there the whole night and waited for the next morning to meet him. It was a cold night, and they somehow managed till morning.

The next morning, they went to see Lionel again.

"Greeting's teacher", they said while bowing with folded hands.

"The visitor's meeting time is 1 pm, this is time for my students' class. You will have to further wait", saying this he started taking his class.

Samuel and Chandrika again went outside of the monastery and sat under the tree.

Now Samuel was distraught. As soon as it was 1 pm, he approached Lionel and said "Is this the right time to meet you now, or do you have to eat now? We both have been trying to meet you since yesterday evening, but you just can't find the right time."

Lionel smiled and looked at him and said, "It was your choice young man, you wanted to meet me hence you came, and you waited. You can't make your choice my compulsion. However, you may tell me the purpose of your visit but before I think you both must have lunch as I'm sure you must be hungry too."

Lionel instructed one of his students to take both for lunch.

Chandrika knew that what Samuel did was not right. After eating, both went to meet Lionel.

"Tell me why you do both want to meet me", he asked

Chandrika replied with folded hands, "I pray that you educate my son in this monastery and make him a great warrior."

"Great warrior!", Lionel replied with a surprise.

That's Ok! But how can I ensure this? He added

"I don't know what you have heard and understood about me and this place. This monastery nurtures the personality and after the completion of education, it's a student's hard work & dedication that they turn out to be. As far as being 'Great' is concerned that depends on extremely hard work, practice, dedication, and sincerity. A teacher is like an anchor who only guides and shows the right path. What we want to become is in our own hands."

"However, both of you introduce yourself and tell, why you want to make your son a great warrior?", asked Lionel.

"Sorry teacher, but I am unable to answer both of your questions", Chandrika replied humbly.

"If this is the case then both of you should leave my monastery at this time because I do not impart my education to the directionless and secret people", he said

"We are neither directionless nor there any secret about us. We are unable to disclose our identities due to ongoing circumstances", Chandrika said, requesting again.

"You may leave, please. When there is no trust and transparency, things don't work out well. And I must know about you before I think of educating your son", Lionel replied.

She kept requesting him, but he disagreed.

"You rightly said it that it was our choice to come here and meet you with our request. You have made your choice not to accept our request and ask us to leave. We honor your instructions to leave from here, but we make another choice of sitting outside and see if you change your decision" she replied, and both sat below the tree again outside the monastery.

The days pass by, they kept sitting there in shivering cold and rain. It was the 7th day when Lionel sent one of his students to them.

"Teacher is calling you", the student said humbly.

The student took them both to Lionel's hut.

"Introduce yourself", said Lionel

"My name is Chandrika and my son's name is Samuel", Chandrika replied.

"Introduce yourself with your real identity because the tolerance which is in both of you cannot be in an ordinary person. I am observing both of you for the last seven days. I have got the answer to one of my questions and I want to know about the other. And now before answering remember, all the choices are with me only", Lionel replied solemnly.

Before she could say something, two students came running and whispered something in Lionel's ear.

Hearing, a deep concern started showing on his face.

Chandrika asked, "Is there any problem, Teacher?"

"Yes, there is. There is a village in the valley wherein people are facing a serious problem for many days now", Lionel replied

"What is it? Please tell me maybe we can help", Chandrika asked showing concern.

"A strange thing is happening in the valley. There is some animal that is killing people, but no one can find who it is. There are only assumptions, at times people claim it to be a Giant Wolf or a tree that attacks the citizens at the night. Yesterday, I sent two of my students to find out and help the villages but just came to know they are being killed last night. I don't know what to do now", Lionel explained worryingly.

"Give me the opportunity, my teacher. I will not let you down", Samuel requested. "If I fail, we will leave from here and will come back."

Lionel looked at him, he was impressed with his confidence & courage.

"But it's very dangerous and you may lose your life too", Lionel replied.

"'A directionless person is dead already', My son needs your guidance to achieve the goal of his life which is far big & huge than this. If this is the opportunity for him, we choose this and are ready", said Chandrika.

"Hmm, I am delighted to see your courage. Please solve the problem of the villagers. It's a deal, if you can do that, I will make you a warrior whose defeat is impossible. I will help you in every way to reach your goal", Lionel replied. "These two students 'Vikram' and 'Neel' will accompany you."

Samuel took Lionel's blessing, asked for permission, and left for the village.

Lionel gave him an 'axe' and said, "You will need it."

Chandrika was happy and believed that her son would surely succeed in his task.

"Now allow me too", said Chandrika, and she started going outside.

"Queen 'Durgashakti'", said Lionel

Chandrika turned around and looked at him in shock & surprise.

"I recognized you on day one, the ring on your finger is the national emblem of 'Thanjavur' that only royalty family has", said Lionel.

"But how do you know this?", Chandrika (Durgashakti) asked

"My father was closely associated with King Virat and had been to your kingdom many times. I am deeply saddened by the death of his son and your husband King Nirvana. Till today, we all had assumed that you and his son were dead, but I was glad to see you on the very first day. I recognized you both. If anyone believed that you are still alive, then it is Markooz, because even today his army is looking for especially you and everyone who could have a runway that night. There is still something bothering him which has not offered him peach even after so many years", he said.

"Samuel's training got started the moment he stepped into this monastery. He certainly has strong willpower and pain tolerance which is the first quality a warrior should have. The given task is not only his test but the source of meeting someone very special and important he would need from now on."

"Queen Durgashakti, I can master him in every martial art, but not in black magic. Hence, he would need 'his' support. Also, there is a secret about Markooz's death which we much find out and there is only one person who can help: Lipika", said Lionel.

"Who is this, Lipika?", Durgashakti Asked

"Queen, it's time for the beginning of the journey too. Samuel would be needing a reply to many of his questions and we both must prepare out self and find the right answers for him", Lionel said. "Please visit Kuntal. Lipika has very important information for us. But remember, you'll have to be vigilant and keep hiding your identity until Prince Samuel is all set to face any challenge. You continue to remain 'Chandrika' for everyone."

"And I think before you leave, you must meet someone very important and close to you. Queen Fiona", Lionel said.

"I...I can't believe she is alive and is here?", Durgashakti stammered. "Oh God, for these many years we believed that she was killed that night. I want to meet her right now, please", Durgashakti said soberingly.

"Of course,", Lionel took her to Fiona's hut.

Fiona was now very old & weak. She could not even remember anything properly. Durgashakti was astonished as soon as she entered her hut. One wall of the hut had a terrifying portrait of Markooz, and the front wall had a portrait of Samuel's childhood as a warrior. On the middle wall is the picture of the battlefield of that dreadful night in which the whole scene of Nirvana's death was captured. There were a lot many faces and images on all sides of the walls.

She touched Fiona's feet, but she looked at her blank.

Durgashakti was very happy knowing that she was alive.

"Now I must go", she said.

Lionel nodded and came to drop her at the monastery's door and said, "Queen Fiona has seen herself how brutally Nirvana was killed. We will soon meet again 'Our next meeting will be here. Good luck with your journey."

Samuel had now reached the village. Vikram and Neel made him meet the village chief.

Chief, in a bewildered voice, told him how a giant wolf comes as soon as sunset and picks up any woman, man, or child who comes in front of him. Many times, people have tried following him but do not know where he disappears.

Samuel assured him of solving their problem and said, "Today everyone must lock themselves inside the house and should not come out before sunrise".

It was sunset and the night began to darken. There was silence in the whole village, and then the chirp of a fox was heard. It was an unusual size wolf. Samuel was following him in secret. Today the wolf was furious because he was not getting his prey. Finding nothing at last he picked up a sheep and took it away.

Samuel followed her very quickly and was surprised to see them. The wolf came out of a cave with his prey and started yelps & howls **ack-ack-ack-ackawoooo-ack-ack-ack.**

Two people came out of the cave. They covered themselves from head to bottom with a long, dirty cloth. Their face could not even be seen because of the darkness. They said something to the wolf in a strange loud voice in anger. The wolf released the sheep buried in its mouth, probably still had life left in it, and the sheep ran away.

It was about to dawn. Seeing that, the wolf first assumed the form of a human, went inside the cave for some time, and came out and stood in the form of a tree in a corner.

Samuel's eyes widened. He couldn't understand what was happening. Now it was sunrise, he moved towards the cave and started looking carefully. He could not see any door in the cave from which anyone could come out. The wolf that had turned into a tree seemed to have been there for so many years.

He returned to the village. All the villagers were looking at him eagerly. He went straight to the Chief's house and said that even today before sunset all the people will lock themselves in their houses and will not come out before sunrise. Even after asking a lot, he did not tell anything to anyone. At the night, again the wolf came, did not find his prey, and went back empty-handed but did not pick up any animal. This sequence of events continued for three days.

On the fourth day, a traveler was passing through that village. It was nighttime. The wolf swung loudly towards him and picked him up. Samuel was asleep when he heard the man's cry. He got up in a panic and ran after the wolf.

The wolf reached outside the cave. As before, two people came out but this time they looked happy. One of them put his hand on the head of the wolf and whispered in the wolf's ear. In no time the wolf killed the man.

The dead body of that traveler had fallen on the ground covered in blood. Then the man turned to smoke and entered inside the dead body lying on the ground. Suddenly the traveler stood up. The wolf converted to man, and they all went inside the cave. Same as before, the man (wolf) came outside and stood in the form of a tree in a corner.

Now Samuel could understand what was happening there and he kept looking at the cave carefully, also waiting for the sunrise.

A voice followed his ears whispering, "What are you doing here?"

He turned around in bewilderment and saw a small man, with a long beard, long ears, a pointed long nose, and only one big eye at the center of his face, was standing behind him. In a panic, Samuel fell.

"I only asked a simple question, there was no need to fall", that small man replied.

"Oh.shit..shit...shit don't you know you just scared me.... I almost got half heart attack", Samuel replied angrily.

"Who are you and what are you're here, what do you want?", Samuel asked.

"Questions, Questions & Questions. But I asked first", the short man said with a cunning smile.

"Answer me before I kill you", Samuel replied in anger.

"Ha...ha...ha...you can't even touch me and if you don't believe may try", the short man replied while irritating Samuel.

They kept arguing for a long and the short man replied, "Oh Come on Samuel, give it a break now!"

In the deep silence, Samuel asked, "How do you know my name?", looking at him.

The short man replied, "I'm Flutus, and have been following you since the day you were here. Let me tell you, you are impressively smart and have well found out what is happening in this village. But what next?"

"Flutus! But why were you following me? What do you want from me?", Samuel asked.

"I don't want anything, nor I was following you. If anyone wants anything, it's you who wants to solve this mystery and solve the villagers' problem. I just thought maybe you need my help, so I came to say 'Hello!'", he replied.

"Oh well thank you so much, but thanks a lot you may go now, buzz off", Samuel replied.

"As expected, I will make a move now", Flutus started walking towards the woods, he turned and said, "Well! Good Luck for tonight."

"Hey, please wait, can you actually help me?", Samuel approached Flutus.

"I know I am a small, tiny ugly man but do I anyway appear to be 'Joker' who cracks jokes? When I said I can help you that means I can", he said.

"I'm sorry for all this, can we talk please?", Samuel requested.

"Better, follow me", Flutus said smiling.

They walked inside the woods and Flutus asked him to narrate the whole incident of last night. Samuel was following him and was narrating the entire incident. He felt a strange thing while he was talking and occasionally looked back. He could see dry and burnt woods but while he looked towards Flutus, he could only see flourishing green with beautiful green trees, plants, flowers, and a fragrant forest.

"So, what have you understood and thought of doing next?",
Flutus stopped, turned at Samuel, and asked.

Samuel looked at him with a loving look.

"What.... why are you looking at me?", he asked blushing

"You are such a wonderful guy, I am having such a wonderful
feeling after meeting you", Samuel replied smiling.

"Thank you, no autographs please! but what is most
important for you right now is to think about the safety of the
villagers, it is going to be dark soon. And whatever you told
me; I have seen it too. However, you have overlooked a very
important thing", Flutus said.

Samuel asked, "Seriously, what?!"

"Let's go to the cave", said Flutus and they both left and soon
reached there.

"Look carefully at this cave and this tree and tell the whole
sequence of events again", said Flutus.

Samuel jumped up with joy and said, "Understood! This tree
is the root of the whole problem. Now I understand why my
teacher Lionel gave me the ax. If I just cut this tree down, the
problem will be solved."

"Oh Boy! I thought you are intelligent but sadly you are not.
Don't see what is visible to everyone, you must focus on what
is hidden. If you cut off this tree you will temporarily be
solving this problem which might occur again one day. Learn
the difference between 'Finishing' and 'Completing' a work!",
Flutus said.

Samuel looked at him confused.

"Let me explain to you", Flutus continued. "One thing is for sure, whatever is inside this cave is not good. Every night wolf only picks the humans but not the animals. Two people who come out are the 'bad spirits' looking for human bodies only to come back to power. As soon as the wolf killed that traveler, that soul entered his dead body like smoke, and he appeared to become alive again, but the 'spirit' has now got a body and must be looking for many more such human dead bodies".

"As soon as the wolf catches a man from the village, he utters a mantra which opens the invisible door of the cave. After the completion of the work, he again closes the cave and stands outside in the cave as a tree and protects it. You are right, this tree is the root of the problem, but it is not its real form. Indeed, its real form is a spirit who turns into a wolf everyone to and attacks villagers to meet the purpose. The spirit needs to be killed a 'wolf' only".

Samuel asked seriously, "How do you know all this?"

Flutus replied with a smile, "You also knew this. You just overlooked a few things and not accessed the whole situation closely. And my friend, there is a logic in every magic, and I know well understand such magics and can perform a bit too".

"So, what is the plan now?", Samuel asked.

"The plan is all yours I can only help you if you wish", Flutus smiled.

"Of course, please! I need your help", Samuel emphasized.

Flutus puts his hand in the bag hanging over his shoulder, takes out a pointed ivory tusk, and hands it over to him.

"What is this for?", Samuel asked.

"This is your weapon. You will need this in tonight's battle or probably in all from now. But remember to use it only when you need it most", Flutus replied.

He further explains, "Now you go back to the village. As usual, all should lock themselves inside and wait for a new sunrise of their life tomorrow morning."

"Tonight, I will be the victim of this wolf and the rest is in your hands now", Flutus continued. "One important thing: don't tell anyone about me."

Samuel nodded and headed towards the village.

"You are a brave and courageous boy, Samuel, who has all the power and strength and handles this situation", said Flutus while he was leaving.

Samuel turned and hugged him.

"Now hurry up, inform the villagers", Flutus said.

It was night, Flutus was walking around the village and waiting for the wolf. Samuel was behind the big rock when the wolf made a loud chirping sound and pounced on Flutus. He picked him up and ran towards the cave.

Samuel ran after him at the speed of the wind and struck the wolf hard with his ax. The blow was so strong that Flutus slipped out of his mouth and fell away.

Now a fierce battle had broken out between Samuel and the wolf, but astonishingly, the faster Samuel was striking and injuring him, the faster his wounds were healing.

Now the wolf also pounced fatally. Samuel's grip on the ax was released, and he fell. The wolf jumped up and attacked him.

Samuel took over and hurriedly threw the ivory tusk around the wolf's neck. Now the wolf was dead and slowly its corpse turned into ashes.

Samuel quickly ran towards Flutus but he was nowhere to be found. He scoured the entire forest till morning but could not find it and went back to the village in despair.

He informed the villagers that the wolf had been killed. The villagers were very pleased, and they offered a lot many gifts to him before he left from there.

On reaching the monastery, Lionel gave him a warm welcome and accepted him to be his disciple.

Samuel was happy but he could not forget Flutus.

Chapter 3: Rise of Markooz

Virat was a very powerful, efficient, and magnanimous prince of Thanjavur. His bravery and beauty were discussed all over the world. His father Ratan Singh was very proud of him.

Virat was skilled in all arts, whether it was martial arts or scriptural policy, he was skilled in all. His country people used to respect and regard him more than his father Ratan Singh. Seeing this his father was very proud and happy. There was deep love between both father and son.

The matter is of those days when Virat was getting an education in the monastery of his Guru Acharya Vishwajit.

Along with all the qualities, Virat was also a great swordsman. With his one blow, he used to cut down any tree and the harshest scripture. His teachers were very happy to see his skill and might.

Virat used to practice fencing every evening in the forest. One day he felt that someone was watching him hide and seek.

"Who is there?", said Virat angrily.

"Maybe you haven't heard, or you don't know me."

"I am asking again, come in front or else no one will be able to save you from my attack", said Virat with a warning.

After scrutinizing the anklets, he saw a very beautiful girl coming from behind a rock.

Her eyes were big & beautiful, her complexion clearer than the moonlight, and shiny long hair. She was so attractive and beautiful as if God has blessed her with all beauty of the world.

On seeing her, Virat got lost in her big and beautiful eyes.

They kept looking at each other for a long,

"I am already dead by seeing your valor and bravery, Prince Virat.", the woman said. "I am here before you, give whatever punishment suits me."

"Who are you? I have never seen you around. What's your name and what you are doing in this dense forest at this odd hour?", Virat asked.

She smiled and said "My name is Amara. I live in this forest. This is my home. Welcome to my home, Prince Virat."

"My home?" Virat exclaimed. "I am the prince of this estate and this forest comes under it too. Anyway, what do you do in this forest, where do you live?"

"You ask so many questions, Prince. No one has any right over nature, Prince. It belongs to everyone", she said.

"But Yes, if you believe that it comes under your kingdom and have all right on this forest, then I hope that you will always take care of it and the people living here."

"Yes, I will", Virat made the firm remark, and both started laughing loud.

"Ok listen, I am curious to know who this pretty lady is.", Virat said humbly.

"I am the nature my Prince which you just promised to take care of lifelong.", Amara said smilingly.

Her reply impressed him, and Virat's mind and heart started attracted to her.

"Anyway, now it's time to go for me. Will meet tomorrow", Amara left in a hurry before Virat could say anything further.

He kept looking at her while she left and till got disappeared from his vision.

With a beautiful image of her in his mind, Virat started walking towards the monastery; he was very happy. He had a strange calmness on his face and a beautiful smile. He was lost in her thoughts all night and now he was just waiting for the next day.

The next day when Acharya Vishwajit was taking a class with students, explaining the strategies & policy in a war; he noticed some change in Virat's behavior. Today he was neither concentrated like every day nor looked interested in the class. He was continuously looking at the sun, waiting for the evening to meet Amara again.

"It doesn't suit a Prince to be so distracted and decentralized 'Virat'. Is there any problem?", Acharya Vishwajit asked.

"Nothing Teacher", Virat said politely.

But you look distracted, lost which is not a good sign! Replied Acharya Vishwajit

"The first duty of a king is to look after and protect his people, the boundaries of the state and nature, animals, birds, trees, and all life. A king should discharge his duties selflessly and without partiality. He can never think only of himself because he has nothing. A 'King' remains a king till his people shower their love and confidence on him. Therefore, it is necessary for a king to always have control over his mind, heart, and all desires.", he continued teaching the students.

Virat pretended to be understanding and listening to what he explained but his mind was distracted.

And finally, it was evening which Virat was eagerly waiting for.

His steps were moving towards the forest at a high speed and soon reached his practice site. His eyes were looking for Amara.

"Will you not practice today, prince?", asked Amara.

Hearing her voice, Virat's happiness knew no bounds.

"Was looking whether someone came to see my practice today or not", he said with a smile.

He looked at Amara, she looked even more beautiful today.

"Of course, Amara is sure of her promise, so you practice now and then we will talk", She said.

Virat showed great agility and force and started practicing his fighting sword skills. Amara kept looking at him in awe.

"Hmm, so my forest queen, would you care to tell me something about you now?", Virat asked

"Have you seen this forest, Virat? Sorry, I can call you by your name, right?", Amara said.

Virat consented with his eyes.

"Well, I come to this forest every day but have not explored it ever", Virat replied.

"That's wonderful. Would you want me to introduce you to your nature? This forest has many beautiful places which I am sure you would love to see", Amara asked.

Virat hesitated.

"What are you thinking? It's alright if you don't want to come", Amara said.

"No, it is not like that. It's just I must go back to the monastery on time, otherwise, my teacher will be angry. But I can manage, so Princess Forest, tell me where we are going today", Virat asked.

She held Virat's hand and started walking towards the forest. It was an electrifying feeling for him, a beautiful feeling he felt in this body from her touch. He went on holding her hand. Amara kept telling him about herself, and places and he kept listening. After some time, both came back to the practice place.

"Now you should go back or else you will have to face your teacher's angry", she said with a smile.

Can I hug you, Virat? Amara asked and before he could say anything, she hugged him tightly.

"Hmm, are we meeting tomorrow?", Virat asked. He only wanted to listen to "Yes".

They looked at each other, though the eyes had already replied, she yes and they both left.

The series went on like this. Both would meet every day. Amara would walk him through the forest, sometimes the river, the mountain, and sometimes the beautiful animals and birds. Both were getting closer to each other after meeting every day. The two used to hang around with each other for hours and spend time together.

One day while both were walking in the forest it started raining very heavily. To escape the rain, Amara took him to a nearby cave, but by then both were drenched. Virat looked at Amara and she started shying away. Two lovers who had not expressed their love to date, this closeness of them did that. Amara was being confined in Virat's arms. It was an expression of two lovers who have everything to each other and had become one.

It was morning and they woke up.

"I have to go, it's too late", said Amara.

Virat grabbed Amara's hand and said, "I love you Amara, and want to go on with my life with you."

She kept quiet and bowed her head.

"Say something", Virat insisted.

Amara looked at him and said, "It is not possible my prince. I can be with you but not your life partner. We can walk together for hours on one road, but our paths cannot be the same. I am with you, today and always, but I do not want to keep any such wish which cannot be fulfilled. You know my prince, there can be no relation between a royal family and an ordinary girl."

"It is not so, Amara, my father loves me very much and he will appreciate my feelings", Virat said.

"Don't be stubborn prince, you also know this is not possible"

"We are in a beautiful relationship, please let it be like this only."

"I must go now", and Amara left.

Days passed, then weeks and months. Virat would go to the forest every evening, but Amara did not come. He would still go to the forest in the hope that one day she would come but it did not happen.

On the other hand, Virat's education was going on and the day had come when he had to leave the monastery and go to his state.

Maharaj Ratan Singh himself had come to bring his son Virat from the monastery to the palace.

Before going to the palace, Virat once again went to the forest in the hope that he would probably meet Amara today.

"Today is my last day here, I need to go back to the state. Are you here, Amara!? Are you watching me? I need to speak to you, please talk to me", he called out.

But Amara was not there, or she did not answer by being there. Virat left in a sad mood but before leaving he left a message for Amara. On a big stone, he wrote with his kukri -

"I have promised to take care of this forest, and everyone lives here, and you have promised to be with your prince always. I will keep my promise and you keep yours". He left.

Amara was there, not only today but every day, but she never tried to meet Virat nor ever answered him.

As the days passed, Amara would wander in the forest sad, she went everywhere she used to accompany Virat. She used to spend hours in that cave and used to feel his love. She had made the cave her home and started living there

One day looking for Amara, her mother Aulika reached the cave.

"What are you doing here, haven't seen you for so long, and neither did you come to meet me?"

Amara looked at her mother with moist eyes.

Aulika consoled her daughter and asked, "What happened?"

Amara clinging to her mother started crying.

She narrated her and Virat's love story to her mother.

After hearing this, Aulika's anger knew no bounds.

"Have you lost your mind? Have you ever seen a human and a demon match? Man is just our food and nothing else. Your job was that you would kill him and eat him instead you fell in love with him. Now sitting in this dark cave and shedding tears like a coward. You are an idiot and nothing else", Aulika angrily lashed out at Amara.

"Mother I have given my everything to Virat", said Amara in a timid voice.

"This is a sin", said Aulika angrily pushing Amara.

Amara fell and started bleeding after hitting her head with the stone.

After all, a mother is a mother, whether it is a human or a demon. Seeing this condition of her daughter, her heart was filled, and she hugged her.

"Does Virat know that you are a demon?", asked Aulika.

"No mother, he doesn't know. I have always met him in human disguise. I also know that after knowing this he will only hate me. But what should I do, mother? I tried a lot to stay away from him. Even when he left from here and kept calling me, I did not even meet him. But now it is getting difficult to stay away from him", Amara said while crying.

"Is there any way mom?", Amara asked Aulika with anticipation and started looking at her?

She kept silent, kept thinking, and said, "There is a way but what will be the result of it in the future, I may not tell."

Amara replied immediately, "I am a ready mother."

"You have to do rigorous worship of our goddess for 51 days, in which you will have to stay hungry and thirsty. Many troubles can come and maybe even your life can be lost. But if she is pleased and blesses you, then anything is possible. One more thing, you will have to inflict a wound on your body from which the blood will continue to drip. While bearing this pain, you have to pray continuously with true faith and sincere values. It won't be easy, Amara", Aulika's explained with a worried mind.

Amara wanted to get her love at any cost and agreed.

"Mother, tell me what and how to do", Amara asked curiously. There was joy and hope in his eyes.

Aulika carefully told her all the procedures, but she was very upset and scared in her mind. She knew what Amara is going to do. If it happens, will be against nature and it will have to face dire consequences in the future. She blessed her and left.

Amara made a strict vow by being hungry and thirsty with true devotion and dedication and on seeing it, 51 days were completed but the goddess did not appear.

She didn't stop and continued to do severe penance, but darkness and despair surrounded her and after 90 days her patience broke, and she started leaving the cave in despair.

Then a voice stopped her, "Ask for a boon, Amara."

The goddess had appeared of amid the blazing flames of the Havan Kund.

Amara's happiness knew no bounds and his eyes filled with tears.

"Thank you for accepting my prayer", she said bowing to the goddess with folded hands.

"Your penance was successful, tell me what you want", said the goddess.

Amara narrated her love story to the goddess and requested her to transform her from a demon to a human.

"But this will have serious consequences in the future, are you willing to face them all? A day will come when you have to choose between your life and your love", said the goddess.

"I am doing all this only to get my love and this all will remain a secret which will go away with my death. May you bless me with the same form and beauty as Virat has always seen me", Amara said while praying to the goddess.

Goddess smiled & said "As you wish, but always remember any work done based on lies is never successful. I grant you all you wish." And the goddess disappeared.

Amara's happiness knew no bounds that she had got what she wanted. Now the only wait was to meet Virat and express her love.

Without wasting time, she sent a message to Virat via her eagle and wrote "A prince had promised that he would always take care of a forest and its nature. Does he remember that promise? Amara."

Six months had passed, and Virat had given up hope of meeting Amara ever again. He kept him busy with the kingdom work and would remember the precious spent with Amara in his free time. His love was still the same for her and continuously made efforts to meet her. That forest was her only destination, he went to that forest many times on the pretext of hunting but could not find her. He had now convinced himself that Amara was gone from his life, but he had an indelible memory of her in his heart.

It was a moonlit night. The whole sky was twinkling with stars. Virat was standing in the window of his room and was looking at his kingdom. He used to do this often. It was such a place of his solitude where he would stand for hours, thinking, remembering the good and bad things of his every day. Sometimes happy and sometimes sad, this was the place where he used to talk to himself.

He saw a golden feathered eagle coming towards him which landed at his window. A dry-rolled leaf was tied with thread in his leg. He could well recognize this eagle as he had seen him many times while walking the forest with Amara.

Wasting no time, he untied the and started reading.

"Yes, yes, yes! I do remember my promises, Amara. How can I forget?", Virat jumped with joy & happiness.

"Like a drowning one with straws"

"Like a ray of light in the dark"

"Like the sun has come out after ripping the dense clouds"

Virat's condition was just like this. Losing himself and regaining again, was the only feeling Virat had.

A big, beautiful smile on the face, love in the heart, a yearning to meet, and tears in the eyes. He rode on a horse and ran towards the forest to meet Amara.

As soon as he reached the forest, the speed of the horse slowed down, his heartbeat was faster. The love of his life, Amara was standing before him.

He got off the horse and his steps started moving towards her.

Virat opened his arms, and she ran and hugged him. Virat tightly held her in his arms. Wiping her tears, he kissed her forehead. They both were happy, very happy!

They spent the night in the cave, and the next morning Virat proposed to her to get married.

"Do you think your father will agree and accept me as I am not from a royal family?", Amara asked.

"You have never told me anything about your family. Can I meet them now? It doesn't matter to me whether you are from a royal family or not, for me, you are the princess of this forest, and my love is unconditional for you. I am sure my father will understand my feelings for you and would agree. So, my love, please don't worry", Virat said.

Amara held her hand and said, "It's only me and my mother in our family. Can you see that mountain? We have a small house there. We do have few cattle and do farming for a living. I did tell my mother about you, and she was so happy to know about you."

Virat smiled looking at her happiness and excitement.

"Would you like to meet my mother, Virat?", Amara asked.

Virat consented with his eyes, and both left for her house. Soon they reach Amara's motherhouse.

"Please wait here. Let me go inside and inform her about your arrival", she said and went inside the house.

Virat kept waiting outside and after quite some time, Amara came outside to take him inside the house,

"Please come in", she asked Virat to come inside the house.

"Oh, Wow! Amazing, Wonderful! What a beautiful house!", Virat exclaimed.

Even Amara was also shocked to see this transformation in her own house. And she could understand the use of her mother's magical powers for this.

Aulika gave a warm welcome to Virat. He was thrilled to meet her and look at the house.

"This...this house appeared to be small from outside but it's huge though", Virat said.

"I am glad you liked it Prince Virat and trust your father will like too. This house is speared all over inside this mountain. Come on, let me take you through the house.", Aulika replied.

Aulika kept showing him the whole house which looked no less than a palace. After a few hours, Virat expressed his desire to return to his kingdom.

"Prince Virat, I am happy that you and Amara are deeply in love and want to get married. If your father does not have any objection and he considers us worthy of this relationship, then I will get this marriage done as per your rituals.", Aulika expressed her thoughts.

"Certainly, I am happy that you respected our love and accepted me. Apart from being a great king, he is also an amazing father who has always taken special care to ensure my comfort and happiness. I am sure he will agree", Virat replied. "I must leave now and will come back at the earliest."

"I will wait for you, Virat. Please come back soon", Amara replied with teary eyes.

He hugged her and left.

The moment Virat left, Aulika's house returned to its original state, a ruin, and herself a witch. But Amara remained a very beautiful girl. She was now convinced that her daughter was now a human, a very beautiful girl whose appearance & beauty has no match.

Talking to the wind, Virat walked towards his kingdom and reached soon. Whoever saw him was astonished. No one had seen him so happy to date and soon Maharaj Ratan Singh got the information that Prince had reached the palace and seemed very happy.

The concierge raised his voice, "His Majesty, The Great Mighty, His Kindness King Ratan Singh is coming".

He had come to Virat's room.

Seeing his father, Virat happily embraced him.

"There is a discussion in the whole state that Prince Virat is very happy as no one has seen him ever. What's the matter son?", he asked in excitement.

"Father, I want to ask you something which you will have to promise you will not deny. I need something which is the reason for this happiness", Virat replied.

"You are the only Prince of this great and huge estate. You need not have doubt. Ask what you want. I can get anything for you. And in fact, I too have great news for you which I am keen to share with you. But first, you tell me what is in your heart", his father replied.

Virat signaled to the guards and servants of his wish to go out.

"I want to get married Father", Virat said to his father.

"What a pleasant surprise! That means you already got the news?", the King exclaimed. "Oh my, I wanted to keep it as a surprise, but someone already told you this", King replied sadly. "But I am happy that you are consented to marry Princess Fiona of Rajgir. She is an intelligent, beautiful, and kindhearted girl. This marriage will also strengthen our relationship with the kingdom of Rajgir and we will have many political benefits. I am so happy my son and looking forward to this wonderful wedding ceremony", he jumped with joy and excitement.

Virat looked seriously at his father. There was silence in the room. He had no idea that his father had arranged his marriage with someone else.

"What happened Virat? Why are you silent? Oh, I understand you wanted to say something, and I got busy telling my things. Come on tell me what you were saying", King said.

Taking a deep breath, Virat said, "I love Amara, a girl I met while I was studying, and want to marry her. She is not from any royal family. She lives with her mother in the Phulkari Forest" and told the entire thing to father.

"Don't you know that you can't marry her? A Prince must marry only in a royal family? How can you even think of it?", King said angrily.

"Please father, please accept my request. I love her. Please grant my wish, I have always and will do everything that makes you happy", Virat requests this father.

They both sat silent for hours. Virat stood in a corner looking at his father.

"A king has the responsibility of his kingdom, and he should not take any such decision in his life which directly or indirectly may affect his kingdom in the coming time. Being a Prince, your decision of getting married to this girl is highly emotional and very personal but as a King, I can't let it affect my kingdom and its prosperity. Even if I agree to accept her as my daughter-in-law, the people of this kingdom may not respect her like a queen. Will you be ok with this?", asked the King.

"Father, she is very beautiful, sharp, intelligent, and carries a great attitude like a Princess. She would quickly learn our traditions and way of living. Her kindness will surely be accepted by our people and would give her the required respect.", Virat kept talking about Amara and convincing his father.

Ratan Singh put his hands on both the shoulders of Virat and said, "I have no one else without you, and today for the first time I have seen you so happy. I do not want to take this happiness from you even if I want to. If this is your wish, I am okay with this. You will be married to Amara, but this Prince will also have to give his kingdom to a queen of a royal family. You will also have to marry Princess Fiona of Rajgir kingdom. And I have already committed for the same."

King continued, "I don't want you to keep Amara in any dark. You must tell her the truth and only if she agrees, you both will be married first." Saying this he left.

The next day, Virat went to meet Amara and her mother and told them everything.

"I want to be with you, and it doesn't matter to me if I get respect as the queen of your kingdom or not. I want to be called your wife rather than a queen. I do understand your obligation towards a second wedding with a girl from the royal family but believe me it will not affect our relationship and I will ensure to give all due respect to Princess Fiona no matter if she accepts me or not. I only expect you to always love and regard me as your life partner". I have made a thoughtful choice my love, Amara said.

Aulika has nothing much to say on this and she only expressed her desire of getting them married for her house to which King Ratan Singh too agreed.

The important and much-awaited wedding day of their life had arrived. Aulika used the best of her magical powers and make an unexpected and outstanding wedding arrangement.

King Ratan Singh and his relatives who had come for the wedding were very happy and impressed looking at their hospitality.

Amara looked as beautiful as ever on her wedding day. It was difficult for everyone to take off their eyes from her. She looked royal and impressive. The wedding ceremony was completed by offering blessings to the couple.

Before Amar started to leave for her new home the Royal One, Aulika took Amara into the house and gave her a wooden box.

"What is it mother?", Amara asked.

"This is a wish box for you, my darling daughter. I know you are going to live a royal life wherein everything will be available in immense but at any point in time if you need to have any specific wish, just ask for it and open this box, your wish will be granted. But remember it should be kept a secret. And never open it unless you have a wish to ask for", Aulika replied rolling her hand on her head.

"Mother, I am sorry. I can't take it. I am leaving behind this life and all magic. I am now and want to live a normal human life", Amara replied respectfully.

On the must insist of her mother she kept it. The moment she touched the box it became so small that she can it kept anywhere secret.

She left with Virat forever a new beginning, a new life.

A few months later Virat got married to Princess Fiona at a royal wedding.

Virat used to spend his maximum with Amara only which was not liked and appreciated by Fiona. She made repeated requests for his time and love, but it was of no use. To keep herself busy and calm she started keeping busy with estate affairs and solving the problems of citizens. This was highly appreciated by the people, and she began to gain much popularity. This made Virat also happy as he was able to spend even more time with Amara as the majority of tasks were taken up by Princess Fiona.

King Ranjit Singh was not much happy about this situation. As he was also getting old, he decided to step down and announce Virat as the King and Fiona as the Queen.

The time pass by, Virat & Amara got blessed with a baby boy which they named "Markooz".

After around a year, Princess Fiona also got blessed with a baby boy which they named "Nirvana".

Both the Prince began growing up together. They always used to share lots of love and care for each other. Virat was a happy father seeing his sons growing up. Neither he nor Amara nor Fiona ever made any distinction between the two princes.

Nirvana had a very calm, soft-spoken, kindhearted, and pleasing personality. He was extraordinarily smart, sharp, fast, and intelligent. As he was growing, he already started to gain popularity among the people. He had a great fan following not only because of this humble behavior but also due to the deep connection of his mother Queen Fiona with the citizens for her active involvement in the estate affairs.

Markooz had tough built, equally sharp, and intelligent but he was slightly cunning, greedy, rude, and selfish. As he grew older, all this increased in his behavior. Often there were fights and arguments with his people. Because he was a prince, people were afraid of him and did not say anything. His desires were also increasing like his bad behavior.

Now, both the princes were 15 years old. They often used to go outside the Palace for hunting, visit the kingdom, and play with their friends.

The behavior of Markooz, which was limited to only inside the Palace, now slowly everyone came to know. He was a prince, so no one could say anything to him hence people started making distance from him. On the other hand, everyone loved Nirvana very much.

Markooz was not bothered by anything. His greed was also reaching its peak. Anything that he liked, he would either pick it up or take it away by force. Nirvana was making his best efforts to control his acts and many times helped him escape, but Markooz has now started enjoying all these things. He found comfort in fearing and troubling people.

This behavior of his was not hidden even from Virat and Amara. Many a time he was explained strictly and lovingly. Everything would remain fine for a few days, but the same behavior would start again.

One day both Nirvana and Markooz were on a tour of the kingdom.

A girl was playing with her white horse. Markooz expressed his desire to ride the horse.

"I want to ride your horse", Markooz said.

The girl looked at him and kept playing with her horse without replying.

"Did you hear what I said?", Markooz said angrily.

"I did but I am not willing to do so, please excuse me. Also, this horse is not ready for a ride now", she replied.

Markooz felt offended and moved toward the girl in anger.

"Stop", asked Nirvana. "We should not force her, please. As she says the horse is not ready for a ride, let's not do it. You might get hurt too."

Nirvana explained to him a lot and took him away, but Markooz's mind was filled with anger, arrogance, and jealousy. That night he planned that would steal the horse. He left in the darkness of the night and reached the same stable where the horse was tied. He went inside secretly and grabbed the horse and started leaving.

"I told you it is not ready for horse riding yet", a voice stopped him from behind.

The same girl was standing behind him.

"Please return my horse, it belongs to me", the girl requested.

This form of Markooz appeared for the first time, his eyes were red like a monster's, frightening face. He turned and hit the girl with both his hands. The bright light emanating from his hands hit the girl and she fell away and became unconscious.

Markooz left from there, but the girl's father was scared watching all this.

This incident spread like fire. There was a whisper amongst the people that Markooz has demon powers. There was an atmosphere of fear all around.

The next day, the girl's father came to King Virat with a request for justice and narrated the whole situation. But Virat did not believe him and assured him all support for him towards the best treatment of his daughter. But he was really surprised and shocked to hear this news about his son Markooz. He asked one of his trusted ministers to secretly investigate the incident.

On the other side, when Amara came to know about this incident, she was much worried and puzzled that how such an incident is possible. She started to fear that some demonic power might have passed down to her son. But she remained calm and did not tell anything to anyone. She also kept convincing Virat that all such news was fake.

This brewing process continued. Markooz used to get everything that he liked in the darkness of the night. It had become his hobby now. He had started crossing the limits of insanity. Many people knew a lot but due to fear, they could not say anything.

Now, everyday complaint were coming to Virat's court.

Sometimes someone's daughter used to disappear and sometimes someone's son. Sometimes someone's an animal, someone's a valuable ornament.

But Fiona was keeping her eye on all the sequences of events. He followed Markooz secretly for several nights, but after a while, he was out of sight.

He did not disappear. He had some magical powers and he used to become invisible when he knew that someone was watching him or was following him.

Day to month and then year to year, discontent and fear were spreading among the people, as well as they were losing faith in their King Virat. Maharaja Ranjit Singh was very sad to see this condition and chaos in his kingdom. He died due to his constant ill-health.

As per the long complaint list in Virat's court, more than 100 girls in the state, more than 200 animals & birds like horses, deer, peacocks, rabbits, and more than 500 valuable ornaments had disappeared, and no one was able to trace them.

One day, Virat along with his two wives Amara and Fiona reached the monastery to meet his teacher Acharya Vishwajit. He told him about all the events that had happened in the last few years and the death of his father. He also showed his helplessness in controlling and handling the situations and requested his help and guidance.

"When you were my student, I told you that a king has nothing of his own, he should give up his vested interests and take care of his kingdom with his true loyalty. You left your people alone with such a big problem for so many years. Even your father left for heaven because of this concern", Acharya Vishwajit said.

"What should I do now?", Virat asked requesting.

"Hmm, sometimes it is wiser to take refuge in God when questions are not answered", Acharya Vishwajit replied. "Organize monolithic worship and chanting of Lord Mahadev for 21 days, which need to be performed by you and your family members only. But note every family member should be present in this worship for all days. Don't delay it, King." With the blessings of Acharya, they all returned to the palace.

"Queen Fiona, I know you are chasing the light in the darkness. At times after walking for long in dense darkness, we see a hope of light. My suggestion would be 'just keep walking' No matter how dark the night is, even the tiniest star glows in the sky. It is also crucial and critical to identifying the right light because not every light illuminates, some also burn the house", Acharya Vishwajit said while she was leaving.

According to the suggestion of the Acharya, the preparation and commencement of the worship had begun.

Markooz was involved in the worship, but he always looked restless. A few days later he began to stay for a while only.

One day he didn't turn up to attend the worship. Amara informed that he is not feeling well and is resting in his room.

But Fiona's mood was turbulent. Not long after the worship began, she secretly headed for Markooz's room. It was dark and he somehow entered his room by dodging the guards, but he was not there.

Fiona was convinced that something was not right. Before she came out of the room, her eyes fell on the light coming from behind a lying screen.

She carefully removed the curtain and saw that the secret door of the room was not closed properly.

During the construction of the palace, an emergency door was built in every room, whose purpose was to protect the people of the royal family in case of any calamity. Through these secret doors, one could safely get out of the palace at the time of disaster without anyone's knowledge. The information and method of opening all such secrets were taught only to the people of the royal family and at the same time, it was also instructed to use them only when needed.

She gently pushed the door and started to follow the way and soon she was out of the palace and was entering the forest. She was scared but kept moving.

She kept walking in the deep silence and began to hear some voices. Along with the heartbeat, the speed of her steps had also increased. Acharya's words were swirling in her mind, "If you want to find something, find the light in the darkness".

As she grew ahead, she saw a big cave inside which was quite bright as if someone had lit many torches.

As she kept approaching the cave, music touched her ears as if someone is dancing and singing in cheer.

She entered the cave carefully and almost stopped breathing as soon as she saw the sight.

Markooz was clad in a tall black and bright cloak. Around him, many beautiful girls were dancing. The surprising thing to note was that they all were flying in the air.

The scene became even more astonishing when she saw that the corpses of many animals and birds were imprisoned in large glass bottles all around the cave. On the other hand, two other men were roasting deer in the fire. Some women were serving liquor to everyone in a rare-looking gold vessel.

Markooz was full of fun and intoxication. Fiona was watching the whole scene carefully hiding. She understood now that it was Markooz who was stealing the people, animals, birds, and other valuable things of the state. He had demonic powers, due to which he has imprisoned everyone and controlled.

Still, there was a question in Fiona's mind. Why all those women are flying in the air? Then tearing through the darkness, wearing white clothes and precious ornaments, a very beautiful woman, dressed like a bride, stands in front of Markooz.

Now, what Fiona saw; she must not have ever imagined. Markooz pulled the girl towards him and took off all her clothes and began to kiss her. He put her on the ground and started to quench his lust.

The surprising thing was that the girl got up in a panic. As if woke up from a deep sleep and started shouting, "Save!", "Save!", "Somebody save me!" Perhaps the effect of Markooz's magic on her was over.

Seeing this, Markooz slit her throat with a sharp knife, and she died. Even more shocking was when he chanted a few mantras out loud, and the girl's corpse disappeared, and she started flying in the air like other women. These were all those girls whom he had killed by making him a victim of his lust. They were all souls he had imprisoned.

Fiona was very scared. She wanted to run away from there, but her legs were not rising as if they had got stuck in the ground. Then someone placed a hand on her shoulder from behind. Not even a single word came out of her mouth because of the fear. Still, she looked back with courage. He was Virat's spy.

He gestured for Fiona to keep quiet and carefully led her out of the cave.

As soon as Fiona came out of the cave, she started running towards the palace with all her life. She now took care of herself, calmed down and sat down under a tree, and started crying bitterly.

That spy also reached there.

Fiona asked in a serious and low voice. "How long have you been knowing this?"

He replied with folded hands, "Queen for the last 8 days only."

"I followed Prince Markooz at night for the last several months but did not know where he used to get lost in the forest. It was only in the last few days that I was able to locate the cave and what happened today I have never seen before", he said.

"Hmm, because he knew that I followed him often. Now that he was aware the palace had organized 21 days of worship wherein everyone is involved, he was sure no one would follow him", said Queen Fiona in earnest. "Now you can go. And yes, don't tell this to anyone until I say", she ordered.

"There is something even more important for you to know my Queen", the spy said while bowing his head

Fiona ordered, "Say what's the matter?"

He sat down on his knees with folded hands and said, "Queen Amara is a witch" and he told the whole sequence of events of how she got transformed into a human. "And if you think that I am lying, then you should separate my head now."

"You can go", Fiona said, and she started moving towards the palace.

She kept walking and tears kept rolling down her eyes and somehow managed to reach the palace back.

All the people of the palace were surprised & shocked to see this condition of her Queen and were upset. Fiona walks toward Virat's room

"Can I come in, my King?", she asked.

It was morning and Virat was in deep sleep, she again called out a little louder, can I come in King.

Virat got up in a panic and reached the door of his room.

"Of course, Of course."

On seeing Fiona, Virat's senses were blown away.

Her hair was scattered, his legs were bleeding, his clothes were covered in soil and his eyes were swollen with tears.

Virat stepped forward and holds Fiona and she tightly hugged him and started crying out loud.

"We have committed a great sin, my king. We could not recognize the killer sitting in our own house. Now what will we answer to our people. We could not protect them, we failed". Fiona kept on crying and talking.

As soon as the news was received from the servants of the palace, Nirvana and Amara also came running to Virat's room, but Markooz was still not there.

No one seemed to understand what had happened and what Fiona wanted to tell.

"Please calm down", Virat said, "and tell me the matter.", while offering water to her.

Fiona held herself up and said "What I am about to tell will have dire consequences, our family will be broken and maybe even the destruction of this kingdom. But as the Queen of this kingdom, I must tell you the truth"

"In the last few years, the suffering of our people has seen hell, they have suffered pain, have suffered a deception. The dignity of women has been tampered with, innocent children, innocent animals have been killed and this work has been done by a person whose duty was to protect each one of them."

Fiona narrates the entire incident that took place last night in the cave.

"Do you want to know, Who the person is?" Fiona asked

"Yes", Virat replied in anger. "Such a person should get a harsh and painful punishment that no one could have ever imagined or even imagined."

Fiona looked at Virat, Amara, & Nirvana and said, "That man is your son, Markooz."

On hearing this, Virat rained on Fiona.

"Don't you know the serious consequences of this accusation?"

"Fiona I never thought that you would be so blind in your jealousy that you would put such disgusting blame on your son. Markooz treats you like his own mother and you have put such a cheap allegation on him. Before saying this, you would have thought about Amara once. She has always respected you throughout her life. She never had any desire to be called the Queen of this great kingdom. She has always considered Markooz and Nirvana as her sons. I feel so ashamed that my family member, my wife, and the Queen of this kingdom, is involved in such dirty politics against her people. I was always aware of your difference about Amara but never thought this will shape up like this", Virat replied frustratingly.

"I have not yet completed, King Virat", Fiona replied firmly looking at him. "It is only the half-truth and today I am not afraid of any consequences even if you pronounce death for me. This is not personal. I am only fulfilling my responsibilities."

"Will you shut up", Virat roared in anger and spoke.

"Sorry, my king but I can't. I have to tell you what you have not known for years. In so much pain I much tell you that you also betrayed in love", Fiona replied.

She took a deep breath, looked at Amara, and said, "Your love of life, Amara is a demon, she lied to you."

On hearing this, Virat lost his cool and took up his sword, and turned to Fiona.

Before, the sword could touch her, a voice approached his ears.

"This is truth, my king"

He was Virat's trusted spy, Parkus.

He was sitting with folded hands, eyes down and down on his knees. "I am guilty of punishment for entering your room without permission, but sir, it is important for you to know that everything Queen Fiona just said is true."

And he told Virat how he chased Marzooz for many nights, what happened in the cave and how so many people of the kingdom were disappearing and what abominable things happened to them. I have enough proof to present in this regard.

Virat still could not believe all this and claimed it was a controversy against Amara and Markooz designed by Fiona.

He went to Amara, looked in her eyes, and said, "Don't you worry about all this, I know this is not true, you can never cheat me. Just say that this all is not true", Virat requested Amara.

Amara held his hand, went down to her knees, and said crying "I was aware that a day will come when I have to make a choice. Please forgive me my love, my king, and my life, I never wanted to cheat you, but I was helpless in my love and situations which I could never change. I did everything just to be with you. What I did may be called wrong, but my intention was always pure. I did it for our love, my king."

She looked at Virat and said, "It's true, I'm a Demon turned Human."

Hearing this, Virat was in a deep shock, darkness started pouring in before his eyes, and he was about to stumble and fall to the ground, Nirvana ran towards him and holds him.

Amara kept requesting him to forgive her and her son Markooz.

There was silence in the room. Breaking the silence, lightning struck the sky loudly, the clouds began to thunder, and stormy rain began to fall.

A similar storm was also taking birth inside Virat. The sadness on his face was now clouded with anger. The trembling voice in his pain had now become a lion-like roar. He got up and ordered his son Nirvana.

"Send soldiers and wherever Markooz is, he should be taken, prisoner. Amara should also be taken prisoner, and both need to be presented in court today to decide on the fate of these two towards their deed. Follow the orders as I say", Virat said and left with Parkus for that cave.

He was completely shattered to see the deed of his son and of the misery that happened to his people. He ordered Parkus to put everything on fire inside the cave and close the entry of the cave forever.

Parkus obeyed the order and he left but the fire did not do any damage to the cave. Everything was the same as before.

On the other hand, the soldiers could not take Markooz as a prisoner. Markooz knew that his truth had come to the fore. He mercilessly put all the soldiers to death.

Nirvana reached Markooz and asked him to appear in court as a prisoner, but he did not agree. He made many fatal attacks on Nirvana and Nirvana only kept on defending itself. He kept pleading with him, but he did not listen.

"I thought I am talking to my brother who will repent after admitting his mistake, but I was wrong, you are just a heinous criminal."

Nirvana strikes Markooz for the first time and a fierce battle ensues between the two. Markooz could not withstand the strong blows of Nirvana for long and was taken, prisoner.

Everyone had come to the court.

Amara and Markooz were introduced. Seeing such condition of his mother, Markooz's anger knew no bounds.

He said to Virat, growling, "My mother has nothing to do with what I did. Free her or else get ready for the destruction of this kingdom."

"You will destroy this kingdom, will you?", Virat replied angrily. "You both are criminals and get ready to face your punishment."

All the people present in the court were told the truth about Amara and Markooz. After knowing that everyone started looking at both of them with disgust. Amara was unable to bear this contempt and hatred, a seed of vengeance had been born in her mind. Now the feeling of revenge had awakened in her eyes too.

Both were sentenced to life imprisonment, with neither food nor water, only 100 whips were ordered every day. If ever they fell ill, not even medical treatment, only to be allowed to die in agony was ordered to be ensured.

To date, no such punishment had been given or heard by anyone. No one had seen Virat so harsh even. According to his order, both were put in jail. This was also ensured that they are not able to escape by using any of their magical powers.

Days passed and then months and years. Amara and Markooz were treated worse than animals. Amara was confident that Virat's anger would subside, and he would accept her again, but it did not happen. She was broken but still loved Virat very much. On the other hand, when she saw this condition of his son, she gets filled with anger. Markooz had become very weak, and could not even sit, and walk properly. Seeing this, Amara's mind started getting very upset and distracted. She did not want to see her son die in front of her.

One day, she remembered that small wish box her mother, Aulika, had gifted her on her wedding day.

"I think the day has come to open that wish box", she said to herself.

But the box was kept in a secret place in her room, and she was also not sure whether that would be there or not by now.

That same night, she gently called Markooz near to her and said in a whispering voice,

"We have to get out of here, my son. I can't see my child in agony before my eyes," said Amara, stroking Markooz's head.

Seeing his mother's faith and courage, Markooz's self-confidence also increased.

"What's the plan, mother?", he asked with a hopeful voice.

"With all your courage and power, hold me on your shoulders so that I can reach the window of this prison", giving courage to him, she said.

Markooz lifted her on her shoulder and led her to the window.

Amara said in a low voice "Can you still hear me today? If yes, then come to me soon, I need your help" and she waited, looking outside the window.

Some time had passed, and the same golden eagle was seen flying and came and sat at the window.

Amara's happiness knew no bounds, she said something in the ear of the eagle, and she flew away.

"Get me down, Markooz", she said.

Markooz was anxiously looking at her, waiting for her to say something.

She smiled and said, "Little more time, my son".

Not long had passed and a small wooden box fell from the window. It was the same wish box that Amra's mother had given her.

"What is it mother?", Markooz asked excitedly

"It's our freedom, my son", she replied.

She gently picked up the box and the moment she touched it, it got converted into a big box.

She opened it very carefully, it was a wooden box with small compartments all around and a crystal ball rolling in the middle. Its door had a mirror where instructions began to appear.

"Ask for your wish", the message appeared before Amara.

She said in a whispering voice, "Can you take me and my son out of this jail?", she said, but nothing happened.

The message again appeared "Ask for your wish."

Amara could understand by now that there must be a procedure to be followed to get the wish granted by this box.

She carefully examined every chamber of the box and she found a dirty torn cloth. She took it out and carefully laid it on the ground and straightened it. The trick to ask for a wish was written on that cloth.

The cloth reads as –

"To gain something, you must lose too,

If one needs to be sent into the light, one must choose to sleep in the dark.

Only one will get a life and the other will have to lose

The one who sacrifices will not go to waste, that one will be able to merge with the light per own wish.

But remember, everything will be according to the law of nature."

Amara could understand its meaning. So, she chose the freedom of Markooz. She chose light for him and darkness for herself.

She understood that she would get out of jail, but as the sun sets and the night begins, her life will also end. She just wanted to spend a nice final and free time with her son.

She didn't tell Markooz anything about it.

Markooz was happy that he was going to be free soon and would live a good life with his mother.

Amara, sought her wish from that wish box as soon as the sun rose, and both were freed from jail.

"Where are we going mother?", Markooz asked excitedly.

"Keep following me", she replied.

She turned at him and asked, "Can you arrange for two horses so that we reach our destination fast?"

"Of course. Please wait here, I will be back at my earliest", Markooz said and left in a hurry.

He went to the same cave where he had imprisoned all the people with his magic. After reaching there, he understood that someone was trying to destroy that cave. But he did not have enough time. He opened two glass bottles and took out the severed heads of two horses and placed them on the ground. He chanted some mantras and two beautiful horses appeared. He quickly started moving towards his mother, but he left, he closed the cave with the illusion that now no one could enter it in any way.

Soon he reaches his mother they started to move ahead.

He asked again, "Where are we going?"

Amara replied, "We are going to your grandmother's house in a far forest so move fast."

"What I have a grandmother too, you never told me?", Markooz replied in surprise.

In a couple of hours, they reached. Before Amara could knock on the door, Aulika opened the door. She was standing with teary eyes.

"I was waiting for you both," she said while hugging Amara.

She was very happy to see Markooz and equally worried to see his health.

She offered delicious food to both of them. With every single bite, their health began to improve. Markooz went to sleep after his meals.

It was late afternoon. Amara was eying sunset.

"What's the matter, Amara? You look worried.", asked Aulika.

She narrated the full incident to her mother and about their escape from jail via that wish box. She requested her to take care of Markooz in her absence.

"You gave away everything for the love of Virat, lost all your powers, did severe penance, remain true to him, and now your life has come to an end. But what you got in return?", Aulika asked Amara.

Amara remained silent. She just asked her mother to make her son powerful because was aware that Virat will come after him.

Now, the last hour was left before the sunset. Amara was sitting on a hill with Markooz. She told him about his father and their love story, her transformation from demon to human, her sacrifice, and her immense pain as he left her. She suggested he should move on with his life and start fresh. Asked him to go somewhere far away. Explained to him that it is good to have power or magical powers, but one should always use them for good. She also told that what he did to the people of the kingdom was inhuman, wrong, and non-appreciable.

"You must see the light", she said and kissed his forehead. "This was the same place me and your father used to sit for long. Here only we expressed our love for each other. Whenever I was weak, helpless, and confused this place has shown me a way out. I wish you make an appropriate and right choice from here and become a good man I should always be proud of."

It was beginning to get dark with sunset. Amara was also getting caught in the clutches of death. Markooz did not know that this was his last evening with his mother. He was patiently listening to her. Both of them were holding each other with teary eyes.

Her breathing slowed down, and her eyes began to blur. Her grip weakened and she fell down the hill.

Markooz tried a lot to hold her, to save her but he could not do anything. He cried aloud and kept crying for hours.

"This is what she chooses for herself", a voice approached his ears, it was Aulika.

"She wanted you to live in return for her life. Life gives every person a chance to make a choice, you also need to choose one. Your mother Amara also made a choice. He chose the path of love and religiously followed it. She gave away everything and today her life too."

"Your father Virat also made a choice", she continued. "He too chose love, but his hatred was more powerful than his love in which your mother has already been burnt and you might also have to. I was wondering if your father was not a king but a common man, would he still have treated his son and wife like you and Amara? He did this because he was powerful and now you have the only choice of becoming more powerful than him, in case you wish to survive."

"You were taken captive and could not protect your mother because Nirvana turned out to be more powerful than you. The news has spread all over the state that both of you have escaped from jail and have been ordered to kill you on sight. The army is looking for you like a hungry wolf who can come here anytime. Will these people leave you even if you go away from here? No, it will not happen. Markooz, you must be strong and more powerful to be able to face every such situation and this is the only choice and option left for you", Aulika finished at last.

Markooz had now made his choice. He stood up, wiped his tears, and roared like a lion.

"This sky, mountains, rivers, waterfalls, trees, animals, birds, and everyone who can see and hear me, then listen. I, Markooz will return one day as the darkness of this kingdom and will swallow everything. That day will have an orgy of death. Blood will flow instead of water in the rivers. People will beg for their lives, but he will only get death. This will be my tribute to my mother", he spoke.

Virat's army was moving rapidly towards Aulika's house in search of Amara and Markooz.

Aulika used her magic and escaped with him. Her house was burnt, and everything related to her was destroyed by the soldiers. A search was made in the woods where Amara's dead body was found.

Virat's anger was so fierce that he even refused to perform the last rites of Amara and her body was ordered to lie in the woods. After searching for a long time, when no news of Markooz was found, it was assumed that he too has died. It was believed due to no food and water in jail for years, he must be weak and while running away, he must have become a victim of some animal.

But Fiona had a firm belief that he is still alive because she had seen the true him. Even Nirvana was also not ready to believe that he is dead or being killed because he too had come to know his power during his fight. It was not difficult for him to defeat him. Hence, it was out of the question that he can easily die.

Time passed by, and Aulika was grooming Markooz as a very dangerous warrior. Now he had become very powerful and cruel. He knew all kinds of art and black magic. Aulika had left no stone unturned from her side.

And one day, Aulika said, "Now you have become proficient in all kinds of fighting styles, and I want you to make your army which ever betrays you, grow your strength, and multiply your power."

Markooz replied laughing, "Then I will have to keep only you and my would-be sons in my army, which is not possible. You want me to get married to thousands of females and wait for my kids to grow and fight for me? Own army! Instead, I should attack the near small kingdoms, win over and their left-out army will be my own."

Aulika angrily grabbed his neck and said, "The leftover soldiers do not make an army, what victory will they give you if they have lost themselves to you? And this is not a joke you are laughing for. Every warrior should have a group of the most trusted soldiers who can never betray him and that is what I am asking you to do."

Markooz asked apologizing, "Now you tell me what to do."

"You have a power that no one has, "magical powers". Anything can be achieved from this", Aulika replied.

Aulika revealed a woman with her illusion and started explaining to Markooz, "Till now you killed all the women you had a physical relationship, you killed each one of her, captured their soul and released after some time. Now you don't have to do that instead keep them with you forever."

"Today I will teach you one last lore by which you can keep the soul of any human being imprisoned and whenever you want you can get them to do any work of yours", continued Aulika. "But that person should come to you on her own else this will not work and may also go against you."

Aulika started explaining, "Look at this woman. We should not force anyone. Being connected is very important in any relationship. Look at this woman, if you think she likes you then only you should approach her and can establish a healthy relationship with her. Never force your hook on anyone. That was your biggest last mistake, you tried to get what you liked with power and coercion, which was and will always be wrong. If you want to become an influential king and increase your power, then win the trust of the people, and respect for yourself in their eyes. Only then will you be able to form a powerful and faithful army that will stand by you in every situation."

She further explained, "Build a reliable contingent of an army that has you and only you."

"I don't understand", Markooz asked in surprise.

Aulika further explained, "Look at this wooden box, it has three shelves, two small and a bigger one. It also has a blue-colored glass at the bottom. Now, whenever you will fall in love with a woman, and she surrenders herself to you and you both reach the climax; hit hard at her heart and imprison her soul. You need to imprison the soul in this mirror, store her heart on the bigger shelf, cut two bunches of her hair and keep it on the rest of the shelves. The moment you close the box, you will have your well-grown sons before you. You must note that the number of hairs in the first bunch will be equal to the number of sons you will have from that girl and the length of hair in the other bunch represents the age of each son from her. All sons of that girl will look alike and will have the same physic and powers. Till the time heart is alive, they will follow as you say but the day heart dies, they all will be standing against you. So, you will have to ensure all safety and secrecy of each of the boxes these boxes."

Aulika performed magic and made him a handsome hunk. On seeing whom every girl used to fall in love with him.

He continued to do as told by Aulika. On seeing it, he formed an army of thousands. He spread such a web of illusion around him that it was not possible for anyone to break it.

Markooz first attacked and conquered smaller kingdoms and then began to subjugate the larger kingdoms. Many kings put down their weapons in fear and many lost their lives. Every day he was becoming more powerful. Now he had a very large army, one which he had created from illusion and magic power and the other which he had conquered all the kingdoms.

The plight of him and his army in the war was not hidden. His elusive army not only used to die but also used to suck every drop of blood from the body of enemy soldiers. There was such an orgy of death, seeing that anyone's soul would tremble.

Markooz was convinced that he was all-powerful and that no one could defeat him. But it was his pride that broke out in the war with the kingdom of Kuntal.

Kuntal was a very powerful kingdom situated in the dense mountains touching the sky. Its specialty was that despite having a very small army, it was very deadly. Their war policy & techniques were so accurate that it was difficult for any enemy to understand. Being situated at a high altitude, this state could keep an eye on the enemy from a distance, so it was very difficult to enter this state.

Markooz had conquered all the states around the Kuntal kingdom, and his goal was to conquer it.

There were two reasons for this. He wanted to make Kuntal his stronghold so that he could keep an eye on all the surrounding kingdoms, and also subdue Kuntal's infallible army.

Following the orders of Markooz, his army attacked the Kuntal kingdom. The fighting went on for many days, millions of his soldiers and skilled warriors were killed but his army could not do anything.

Now Markooz went to war alone. He rode on a horse and went ahead at a high speed, whoever came in front of him would be put to death. He was just approaching the gate of the palace when a big arrow pierced his chest and he fell to the ground. The arrow was fired so fast that it had passed through the body of Markooz.

He got up and found the princess Lipika of Kuntal standing in front of him. She was a very skilled warrior, an expert in red-hander and archery, she was faster than lightning.

Lipika, holding the sword, started making big and deadly strikes toward Markooz. He was astonished to see her. He had already laid down his arms in front of her beauty.

She kept on attacking and Markooz got injured badly, then his elusive army reached and protected him and took him away from the battlefield.

He lay wounded on the bed, but Lipika's beautiful face could not be removed from his eyes. Soon he recovered and sent his own general, Haliba, to take his marriage proposal to Lipika.

Lipika turned down the offer and wrote in response "Markooz is a slave defeated in war and his only place is in my feet. Even I had defeated him in war. I will never marry a cruel person. I order you to leave our kingdom with your army in the coming seven days forever and go far away otherwise the eighth day will be the last day of your life".

Reading Lipika's, reply he laughed out loud, laughing out loud. But now there was anger on his face. His eyes had turned red.

With his elusive power, he laid such a perfect trap that no one could even see him while entering the palace. With a sword in both his hands, he entered through the gate of the palace. He was invisible, no one could see him and all the soldiers standing on the guard were being killed.

There was a stampede in the palace due to the screams of the soldiers. It was during the night that Lipika got up in a panic and took out her sword and came out of the room. She saw that the soldiers who were guarding were being throttled and they were falling. She understood that someone elusive had entered the palace.

Both her brothers were also killed in front of her eyes. Markooz's sword was raised towards his father and Lipika shouted,

"Stop, Markooz. Please leave him", in a painful voice she pleaded.

"I'm impressed, no one could see or recognized me, but you have. I don't know you love me so much", Markooz replied laughing. "Princess Lipika, how can you request a slave?". He grabbed Lipika's father's neck in his hands.

She pleaded again, "No...no...no... please I request you, let him go. I will do as you say."

Markooz held him by the shoulder and said, "Where is your attitude today? Where is that pride? You have only two ways - first, marry me. Second, command your invincible army that from now they will follow as I say. And yes, my darling princess, don't ever try to play smart or trick me, unnecessary your dear father will lose his life."

Lipika had no choice but to accept.

Markooz married her and became the king of Kuntal.

He was becoming powerful and never, but he could forget the fact that once he was defeated by Lipika.

And one day he went to Aulika,

"Greeting's grandmother!"

Aulika was delighted to see him.

"You look stressed", she asked.

Markooz sat next to him and said while looking at her, "I have gained lots of power and have formed a huge army but still I could get defeated in the war. I am afraid that a day will come when I can get killed and I don't want that to happen to me. Is there a way I can defeat death?"

Aulike smiled and replied, "You are asking something impossible. The one who takes birth must die as well. No one can change the law of nature."

Markooz, further insisted, "There must be a way out! You have so much power, can't you do something on this, please."

Aulika took a deep breath, "I can't make you immortal. But, yes, there is a way that death can't touch you easily."

She kept on telling Markooz how to conquer death and he kept following the instructions. In the end, she gave him a four-horned horse and instructed him to ride only on it from now on.

At last, she said, "Remember, you can only beat death as long as it is just a secret."

He took blessings from Aulika and started leaving.

After two steps he stopped, and with the sharp strike of his sword, severed Aulika's neck from the torso. Her head fell to the ground, and she died.

"Secret is now actually a secret, grandmother", and he started laughing out loud.

And he left.

Chapter 4: The Journey of Samuel

""I am very happy with your bravery and now I want you to start your training to achieve your goal", Lionel said.

"What is my goal teacher?", said Samuel seriously.

"Your country Thanjavur is living in darkness for centuries. You must give it a new direction and dawn. People there are eagerly waiting for their prince to come back, save and free them from the tyranny of Markooz & people", Lionel explained to him.

"But now we have no one here. That night we and all our people lost their home, property, lives of our people, and our self-respect and left the same". Tears welled up in Samuel's eyes.

Lionel placed his hand on his shoulders and looked into his eyes and said, "There are many people out there who are suffering their humiliation, insult, and tyranny every day only in the hope that one day they will get justice. They will get their revenge for the humiliating death of their people. Their houses were burnt to ashes in a jiffy, that fire is still burning in their hearts".

"A fire is burning in my heart too, teacher, I still remember that night, the way my mother protected not only our family but the entire people. My father died on the battlefield while breathing his last. I could not even see the last of my father. Defeating and killing him was not possible for Markooz and certainly, he was cheated in the war. "I know my goal and duty, and I have been preparing for war for the last many years. My mother feels that I am wasting my time by roaming in the forest, but it is not that I have practiced a lot and I have made myself tough & strong. All I need now is your guidance and learning of war diplomacy. From the death of my father, I have well understood that it is not enough to be powerful only to uproot the empire of Markooz", Samuel replied.

Lionel put a hand on Samuel's head and said, "You and your mother have faced adversity and exhibited an amazingly tough personality. Your journey will be challenging. You are right that just being powerful is not enough, the coming war will be very fierce for which you need enough weapons, education, art, and skill."

"You must start now, said Lionel, pointing a folded paper towards him. This is where your journey starts, and this paper will keep guiding you further. Remember one thing, you will find many people as you proceed, be wish enough to recognize 'a friend' and 'an enemy'", Acharya said.

Samuel sought his blessing and left.

Lionel had given him a map. He had to go to a water palace located within the Mediterranean Sea, located in the north.

He set out and after traveling for several days reached the coast of Malta. Coming there, his map was also completed. It was a huge ocean, and he could not understand where to find the water palace now. He saw a narrow path leading to the ocean. Excited, he ran towards that and then he collided with something and fell away after falling. Surprisingly, there was nothing on the road that he could hit. He stood up and moved forward again but once again he collided with something and fell away.

Now he was angry, he ran again and then a voice came behind him.

"You won't be able to. Let it be"

Flutus was standing behind him and laughing loudly.

Samuel was surprised to see him and was very happy in his heart.

"You! what the hell are you doing here? I thought that wolf killed you", Samuel said.

"Well, this is not possible, and you are such a mean friend, did not even find me and left me there", Flutus said while complaining.

"It is not like that, really searched for you till morning but you were nowhere to be seen."

"Anyways, what were you doing? Can't you see that huge fat man, you are falling again and again by hitting his tummy? Can't you be careful? Silly boy! Flutus said.

Samuel looked at him in surprise and said, "It's nobody."

"Oh, then you must be fond of falling", said Flutus with a laugh.

"Will you tell me what to do now, rather than making fun of me", said Samuel.

"A big fat man is standing there who has blocked the way to go. The important thing is that he can't see in the daylight, he is moving his legs to the right and left very quickly so that someone can't pass through. Twice you collided with its fat belly and fell far", Flutus told.

"And how about night?", asked Samuel.

"Well, In the night he will make your bones a puddle because he can see", said Flutus.

"Oh... we have very little time, but I can't see him, what to do?", Samuel mentioned.

Flutus held her hand and said, "Close your eyes." A light blue color light coming out of Flutus' hands started absorbing Samuel's hand. He said, "Now you can open your eyes". Now Samuel could see that man blocking the way.

"I can see him now but how this is possible", he said excitedly.

Flutus was smiling looking at her. Samuel ran to him and hugged him. "Why do you always come to help me? Who are you?", asked Samuel.

"You can consider me your friend. We have both set out on a journey and perhaps our destiny is with each other. Now your path is clear, go ahead but remember that even if you accidentally come between his legs, then your death is certain", Flutus cautioned him.

Samuel stepped forward and hurriedly crossed the path between the fat man's legs and moved on. He had now come closer to the ocean. He saw that a girl was doing penance on the shore of the sea. It was covered from all sides by a thick sheet of sand.

He started moving forward without disturbing her, but he would go from any direction, that girl would come in his way every time.

"Why are you blocking my way?", said Samuel.

Saying this another girl like him appeared in front of him. As many times as he asked, another girl would appear in front of him. Now nine such girls had come in front of him, and he was not able to move forward.

It is a sham and nothing else, the easiest way to eliminate any fear and confusion is to go on with courage. No matter how big the trouble is in front, we can easily defeat the courage of the other person with our courage and courage. "Don't look at that girl and keep moving forward", Flutus said.

Samuel did not stop walking. He went on and now he was in the sea. He was searching the Castle and a huge octopus came dancing in front of him and blocked his way.

"Why did you come to my street, making me upset, go back... go back soon else you may die", Octopus asked singing.

The octopus attacked him, but nothing could harm Samuel.

"If you don't want me to kill you, then tell me, have you seen any castle in this sea?", Samuel asked.

The octopus laughed and said "Yes, I have seen it, why didn't you ask earlier" and started laughing.

He jumped up and stood in front of Samuel with all his legs spread and said, "You are brave. Now it remains to be seen whether you are wise or not. I have a door in each hand, if you can find the right door, go to the castle. And, if you can't do that, then put your head in my mouth by yourself so that I can eat you easily", said the octopus.

Samuel agreed and began to find the right door.

As Samuel chose the wrong door, the octopus chuckled loudly. Now there were only three doors left. When Samuel looked towards the mouth of the octopus, inside which he saw the shadow of a castle. He understood that the real door was in his mouth.

Now Samuel reached his fifth foot of the door and pointed to Flutus. Flutus quickly jumped and stuck the bone of a big fish lying on the ground in the mouth of the octopus, so that he could not close his mouth. They both jumped inside his mouth and went to the other side. Soon they reached the castle.

Samuel was surprised to see a man amputating his leg outside the castle.

"Why are you sitting here & cutting yourself down?", asked Samuel.

The man replied, "There is a princess inside the castle whose frog has been lost. I couldn't find that, so I got this punishment and he kept cutting his leg."

Samuel was about to enter the castle when a message appeared on his map, "The sword has a sharp edge. It is a swindler, it takes life easily, you will fall in love with your hand at the right time. If you make a mistake, your neck will be cut in a moment".

Samuel stepped forward. There was a big and high throne in the middle of the castle, and the girl sitting on it was weeping sobbingly. He was fascinated by the sight of her, she was very beautiful, dressed in beautiful clothes, with a crown studded with a lot of jewels and precious stones.

"Ahm...Ahm...can I help you princess?", Samuel asked cleaning his throat

The girl looked at him and said, "Can you?"

"Of course.... why not? Tell me please what I can do for you my beautiful princess", Samuel replied.

"Oops flirting has started, don't get confused and see if there is any other message on the map", said Flutus whispering in his ear.

"What is this small man whispering in your ears?", Princess asked.

"Well, nothing it's his regular habit to just keep bothering me, please ignore", Samuel replied.

The princess moving towards him said, "My name is Julie. I am the only owner of this castle, here I and my little frog live together but since morning he is lost somewhere. I can't live without him can you please help me finding him". She started crying out loud.

"Hai...please don't cry. I will find him for you. Please tell me something about it so that I can recognize him", Samuel said.

"Oh...thank you so very much, you are so kindhearted, smart, handsome, and tough too", Julie said winking her eye.

"My frog has bright green color, big eyes, and a beautiful smile, he is wearing a red color jacket, "a real cutie", please find him", she said requesting and started singing and dancing.

"I am Julie, the princess of this beautiful castle, if you find frog & make me happy, I will shower by beauty on you", she kept dancing & singing.

Samuel then saw that the Frog was shining his face with Julie's crown. He grabbed the frog from his neck. Julie grabbed her neck too as if she started to feel suffocating. Suddenly it turned into a big cupboard and the frog turned into a big iron key.

Samuel opened the cupboard with the key. Inside it was a sharp gold sword. As he picked up the sword, the man sitting outside the castle who was cutting his leg turned into a dragon and began attacking Samuel. A fierce battle ensued between the two.

Samuel killed him with the sword. As soon as the dragon fell to the ground he turned into a soldier and bowed down to him and said "I am glad that you own this sword, you are a great one. It is not an ordinary sword, no one can escape its blow and it can attack anyone by taking the form of a person, animal, or any weapon. You have achieved this with great wisdom and bravery, but May I ask you a question? I frightened you at the entrance but still, you came in, why? Many people came before to take this sward but either they ran away out of fear or got into the trap of Julie."

"A castle water and its only princess is not possible. Also, no matter how extreme the situation, it is very difficult to harm yourself. It was strange that you were hurting yourself so easily and hurting your own leg. I understood that this is just an illusory trap and nothing else", Samuel said.

"But tell me one thing, who hid such a mighty sword here underwater and how you are here", Samuel asked.

"Centuries ago, there was a great priest named 'Yadvendra'. He was a very majestic, scholar, and a knower of Vedas. By doing severe penance, he manifested many powers with his knowledge and knowledge of Vedas, through which he used to help and help people. But this thing was not liked by the 'Drishtudum', king of the estate. He asked a priest to use all his powers and knowledge for increasing his glory, destroy enemies and make him powerful. But this was not acceptable to him because he knew that the king would misuse his powers. On this, the king became angry and started troubling him, but he could not stand before Yaduvendra's powers."

"The king knew black magic and hatched a conspiracy so that he could kill Yaduvendra. Due to this, he started to remain weak and very ill. But to fight back he kill the effect of the king's magic, will all his knowledge of Vedas he created a sword that could destroy any kind of power, especially black magic."

"The king came to know about this and tried his best to get that sword, but he could not do so. One day when the priest was sleeping, the king tricked him into black magic, which caused termites to enter his body. Soon, almost the entirety of his body was destroyed by termites. He was worried that if that sword fell into the hands of the king, he would misuse it a lot. He called one of his disciples and requested that he should hide his sword somewhere so that it could be fined or misused by the king or any other wrong person."

"The disciple was equally worried about his teacher and hid him along with his hut and sword in the depths of the ocean and promised that he would protect him as long as a true-hearted, fearless, and powerful man doesn't find it to accomplish a good goal."

"This castle is nothing, but the hut of that priest and I am the same disciple", saying this he bowed to Samuel and disappeared.

Samuel was delighted to learn that he now had a weapon with divine power. He along with Flutus started coming out of the sea and soon came to the shore.

A message popped up on Samuel's map, "You have to go to that place where the essence of your life is, a flying bird is waiting for you. Touch the heights and go beyond the mountains."

Next destination "Thanjavur".

He was surprised. On hearing the name of 'Thanjavur' in his childhood that dreadful night came before his eyes. His pride became restless, and his eyes turned red with anger. Maybe he was waiting for this day. He kept staring at the map.

"What happened Samuel?", asked Flutus.

"It's time to move on, let's start the journey", said Samuel and he left. They followed the map and reached there after four long days.

"Mazar?", Samuel said in astonishment. He saw a large placard on the main gate of the kingdom with 'Mazar' written on it.

"How this is possible? The name of this kingdom is 'Thanjavur' but here it is written as Mazar", said Samuel.

"Didn't your map bring us to the wrong place? And how come you are so sure about it? Have you been here before?", Flutus replied.

Samuel looked at him and then towards the city, "Let's go inside, we are at the right place."

He could recognize his own country no matter he was very small when he left.

There was a strange quickness in his feet, a gleam in his eyes, and a pounding heartbeat. He went ahead and quickly reached the city. Nothing was the same as before. The clothing of the people had changed. 1The appearance of the city had also changed. He had become very emotional after coming to his hometown and tears started pouring down his eyes.

Flutus kept looking at him and continued to walk along.

A loud voice approached their ears, "Be careful, the king is coming, keep the way clear."

Samuel's steps stopped. He had never thought that he would meet Markooz so soon. He had never seen him but had a cruel image of him in his mind. He was ready to see him first.

A trembling voice said softly "Low your eyes and when King 'Zain' passes by you, say loudly 'Long Live King Zain' or else you will lose your life for no reason."

He turned and saw an old woman standing behind him.

"King Zain!", Samuel said in shock, "I thought Markooz…"

King Zain's patrol started passing and all the people, lowering their sights, stood up and started hailing him.

Samuel could not understand how 'Thanjavur' became 'Mazar' and the king is 'Zain' instead of Markooz.

After the king's departure, both of them also moved forward.

"Wait", said the same old woman, stopping them both, "Who are you?"

"How does it concern you?", answered Samuel.

"Tell me who you are. Or should I tell the soldiers that intruders have come to the city?", the old lady replied.

"What do you need?", said Samuel slyly.

"The answer to my question. Who are you two?", said the old lady.

Without replying to her they moved forward.

"There is no one here who even dares to take the name of Markooz. Who are you?", the old lady asked again.

Samuel understood that he had come to the right place and that this old lady could clear all his confusion.

"Can we go somewhere else and talk? There are many people here and I do not want to answer your questions here", Samuel said to the old woman.

"Hmm….", she nodded and said, "Follow me."

Both went after her and reached a stable Seeing so many horses, Flutus asked curiously, "Whose are these beautiful horses and such a big stable?"

"Keep coming in", said the older woman sternly.

The old lady took them to a hut and closed all the windows and doors.

She took out a big and sharp knife and with her trembling hands placed it on Samuel's neck and threateningly asked "Now tell me who you are and how do you know Markooz. And remember that even if you tried to lie, this knife will be across your neck."

Flutus laughed and said, "Really!?"

"Flutus, quiet!", said Samuel.

"There is no fear of Markooz in your eyes, if anything, then a lot of hatred and anger for him. I can immediately kill you with your knife; so, it would be better if you take your knife from my neck", said Samuel to the older woman.

The old woman put the knife in Samuel's neck and said, "Don't even try, because I am old but not weak. My people have come out of this hut, if you hit me even a scratch, your death is certain." Then she glanced at the map tied to Samuel's waist, and the knife fell off from his hand.

"Are you from the royal family of King Nirvana?", the old woman asked crying.

Samuel was surprised by her question. He held her gently and asked "First of all, it is important for me to know who you are.

Who has so much hatred for Markooz and so much sympathy for Nirvana?"

"My name is 'Vashi'. This is my country, my home. But many years ago, a savage rascal destroyed everything. People's homes, their lives, this entire city, and this country were destroyed in a few moments. I saw my father dying in front of my eyes. He burnt my house, raped my sister, and even broke my leg. If I am alive today, just to see his end. I can't forget that night, his cruel smile. I just want to hear him scream in agony."

She kept on talking and Samuel was listening. Tears were pouring out of his eyes and there was a lot of pain in his voice.

"Is he Markooz?", asked Samuel.

Vashi nodded and replied, "Yes."

"The actual name of this state is Mazar and not Thanjavur. Here was the rule of a great majestic and generous king Virat. He loved his citizens like his own children. Our queen Fiona took care of everyone like a mother. But I don't know how a demon took birth in the house of such a great king who was none less than a God. Markooz was the son of Amara, the second wife of King Virat. He had two sons, Nirvana and Markooz and both were opposite of each other. Nirvana was a benevolent, man of good character, on the other hand, Makrooz was insidious, cannibalistic, and cruel."

"It is heard that his mother Amara was also a demon who married King Virat fraudulently. When he came to know about this, he punished his wife Amara and son Markooz. He avenged the same and attacked this kingdom and killed our brave king Nirvana by deceit and destroyed the whole city and gave it a new name Mazar."

"But how come the king is Zain?", asked Samuel.

"He is the son of Markooz, even crueler than him. He inflicts a lot of oppression on the people. If someone lifts his eyes and looks at him, he gets their eyes removed."

"Why did he cut your leg?", Samuel asked.

"My father had a famously stable and our horses were famous for their best quality and characteristics. This is about the days when both the prince Nirvana and Markooz were young around fifteen years. They often used to visit the city for sightseeing. One day the two princes walked to our stable and Markooz expressed his desire to ride one of our horses which I was playing. The horse was not ready hence I denied but he felt bad."

"After a few days, he tried to steal that horse in the dark of night, but I caught him, he got angry and attacked me. A bright blue light emanated from his hand, and I fainted. I regained consciousness after twenty days and when I woke up my leg was amputated. Slowly the horses started disappearing from our stables. One day my father came to know that Markooz stole them and takes them to a cave. When my father protested, he hanged him and killed him in this stable. He had started liking my sister Sylvia, but she knew that he had killed our father and that he was a scoundrel, so she stayed away from him. One day Markooz forcibly picked her up and took her to the same cave, but she ran away. He raped and killed her in front of my family. Markooz gets what he wants, either by theft or by force", Vashi said.

"But...How will you get your revenge on him?", Samuel asked.

"The night our king Nirvana lost his life to protect us, our queen Durgashakti protected all of us, she asked us to come with her to a safe place. Many went with her, and many decided to remain here. She promised she would come back for the justice of all of us. I trust she will keep her words because even when our king was taking his last breath on the battlefield, the first queen performed her duty and protected everyone", Vashi added. "You have asked me everything but haven't told me who you are yet", said Vashi.

Samuel looked at her and said, "I am Samuel, the son of King Nirvana and Queen Durgashakti."

On hearing this, Vashi's happiness knew no bounds.

"I knew our queen would fulfill her promise. Seeing that map with you, I understood that you are from the royal family of Nirvana", she said crying.

"But how have you come here alone? Where is Queen Durgashakti?", Vashi asked.

"Maybe it's not time for her to be here."

Samuel showed Vashi the message on his map and asked, "Can you understand what it means?"

"Your destiny has brought you to the right place, son. Someone has been waiting for you for a long time, come with me", said Vashi.

She opened the door of the hut and began to move. They walked inside the forest and soon reached a mountain. She made a voice 'ah...take...take...tak'. A beautiful white horse flying from the sky landed in front of them. It had beautiful, feathered wings.

"This is your flying horse", Vashi said smiling. "These are very rare species which my daughter discovered. One specialty about them is that we don't choose them, rather they choose us. Go near the horse and try riding. If it allows you, it will be with you till eternity."

Samuel touched the head of the horse and kissed it. He caressed her wings lovingly and patted her back.

Samuel got down on his knees and put both his hands in front of the horse. The horse felt consciousness in his hand through Samuel's affection. Samuel rode on him and the horse carried him into the sky. Vashi and Flutus were looking at both happily. They soon returned.

"Give him a name, Prince Samuel", a voice said.

Samuel turned and saw a very beautiful girl standing with a bow. She bowed down to him.

"Who are you?", asked Samuel.

"She is my daughter Purva", said Vashi.

"This is no ordinary horse. He can fly at high speed in any weather. Can be invisible and can float underwater. No other horse can beat its speed", said Purva.

"Thunder seems to be the best name for him then."

"Thank you very much. A skilled ride is very important for a warrior. I am glad to have him", Samuel said to Vashi and Purva.

"Along with the ride, a skilled charioteer is also very important. He can also prove to be decisive in the war. I think you should meet a great charioteer before leaving here", Purva said.

"From whom?", asked Samuel.

"Parkus", said Purva.

"Is he alive? I thought we lost him too like my father", Samuel said in excitement.

"Let me introduce you to him, he will be very happy to see you. Come with me", Vashi said.

Samuel, Flutus, Vashi, and Purva began to walk through the forest, and quickly into a cave at the bottom of a mountain. As they continued, a noise was reaching their ears and was getting louder and louder.

They saw about thirty to forty warriors holding a warrior under themselves and attacking him hard. Many more warriors were shouting slogans around him 'Parkus', 'Parkus', 'Parkus'.

Then the warrior got up and threw all the other warriors in the air. He was 'Parkus'. Long thick hair, strong stature. All the other warriors were falling away from his one blow. He was very powerful. He could not be controlled by anyone.

'Parkus' looked at Samuel and said, "Welcome Prince Samuel. Greetings!"

"Don't be surprised, I have been keeping all news about you and queen Durgashakti for a long. Hope you had a comfortable journey to your home back", he added.

Samuel with teary eyes went to him and hugged him. "I am so glad to see you", he said.

"Tears do not suit a warrior's eyes, Prince, tears are a sign of weakness. Our goal is very big and hard, in which these tears have no place. All these people you are seeing standing near you, their eyes have dried up and now they have only embers in their eyes. The only desire left in their heart is the enemy's blood. We all have sacrificed our every sorrow and formed a strong army, which you now have to lead", Parkus said.

"But before that, you must prove that you are even worthy to lead us or not", Parkus added.

Everyone, looking at Samuel, touched the feet of 'Parkus' and looked into his eyes, and said, "The one who is standing before you, is the son of a great warrior you all know as Nirvana who stood alone on the battlefield to save the lives of his people. He stood and fought till his last breath. I don't know what this fight is for all of you. This is a duty for me which I will also perform till my breath. Tell me what I am required to do?"

"There is a province attached to this state whose chieftain is 'Kalazi'. You have to kill him. It is believed that 'Kalazi' has some such deadly powers, which can easily destroy any kind of black magic. The continuance of all his powers lies in the garland he wears around his neck. Whoever gets that garland is sure to win over all his powers", Parkus said.

"Markooz attacked the 'Kalazi' several times, but he was never able to defeat him nor could he gain power", Parkus added.

"But Markooz is so powerful, how could he not defeat him", said Samuel in surprise.

"He is an insidious, cowardly and greedy person. To call him brave and powerful is also an insult to valor", said Parkus angrily.

"Kalazi is a brave warrior who is skilled in sword fighting and wrestling, he cannot be intimidated even by magical powers because he is his own master", Parkus added.

"Then how will be he able to defeat him, I mean to kill", Flutus asked.

Parkus looked at Flutus and said, "It will be difficult but not impossible."

"Prince Samuel, you have been working hard and practicing in the woods for many years," said Parkus. "I and my spies have seen your practice, if Kalazi is powerful then you have amazing agility and you are also powerful. You just need to learn a few tricks that I'll teach you", said Parkus

"Can I ask you a question?", Samuel asked.

"If the question is that, how do I know so much about you, then when the time comes, you will get the answer to every question. Right now, you must prepare for the war with 'Kalazi'", said Parkus.

"So, what is the plan?", Samuel asked.

"The gates of the province of Kalazi open only three times a year. Once before the onset of winter, the second time before the onset of summer, and the last time when he organizes a competition to recruit new soldiers and bodyguards into his army. And only during the competition, outsiders are allowed to enter the province. Many warriors rs from all over the world join him to get a place in his army because he gives them abundantly everything that a human being craves like money, good food and drink, valuable clothes, weapons, and beautiful girls. But if anyone makes even a small mistake in the security of the province, then his punishment is only death", Parkus said.

"The next competition is after three months in which you also must participate. Till date, who has not challenged 'Kalazi' to war by entering his own province, but you need to do so. You will challenge him to a wrestling battle. He is a brave warrior he will definitely accept your challenge", Parkus added.

"Hmm", Samuel nodded his head.

Parkus extended his hand to Samuel and gave him a ring saying, "Welcome to your country, Prince."

"This is a sign of our royal family", said Samuel excitedly.

"This ring belongs to your father, Prince who was waiting for you till today", Parkus said.

Samuel embraced Parkus, his eyes moist and a smile on his face. He thanked him.

"Now take rest, you must be tired from the journey. Your practice will start tomorrow", Parkus said.

Vashi said in excitement, "Today there will be a celebration in the joy of Yuvraj's arrival."

It was evening. Delicious food and concerts were held to celebrate Samuel's arrival.

The next morning Samuel invited Parkus to his practice area. It was a small hidden plain of a forest, surrounded by thick, big, and strong trees. Between it was a long, cylindrical, and strong mountain of hard stone.

"Can you break this mountain with your single stroke?", Parkus told Samuel.

"How is that possible, what a huge and strong mountain it is", Samuel replied in astonishment.

"I didn't ask you for the analysis of the mountain. My question is whether you can break it with one blow or not", Parkus replied.

"Of course,", Samuel replied in a confident voice.

"Good, go ahead and hit", Parkus said.

Samuel rushed forward and struck the mountain with all his might with his right kick. As soon as he struck, he sat down holding his leg and started moaning in pain.

"Arise and strike, until you are told to stop", Parkus said giving orders.

Samuel got up and continued to strike, but not a single pebble of the mountain moved, but Samuel's leg was bleeding. He did not stop and kept on hitting till he got tired and fell to the ground.

Parkus asked two of his soldiers to take him to his resting place and to apply medicine to his wound. Seeing this condition of Samuel, Flutus was very disturbed, and his eyes were moist. It was late evening, Parkus came to Samuel and asked him to rest after eating. At the same time, he was asked to come again to the training site the next morning and left. Samuel groaned in pain for a long time and fell asleep. Flutus served him all night long.

The next day Samuel arrived at the practice site and again Parkus asked him to break the mountain with his blows. He continued to strike with both his feet without stopping. Both his legs were bleeding and swollen but he did not stop. He became angry and continued to strike with all his might. As his pain increased, so did his anger. Now he started hitting with punches and both the legs. Blood started to flow from both of his hands and legs. But he continued to bear all the pain, did not stop, did not give up. It has begun to dark, he came back to his resting place and slept. Flutus again served her all night, applied ointment to her wound, and kept crying while looking at him.

The next morning, he went again, Parkus again asked him to do the same. It had been eight days since this went on. Now Samuel's anger had subsided, and he was constantly trying to break the mountain somehow. But still, not a single pebble of that mountain had moved. It was evening and Samuel went to his resting place and slept after having dinner. His condition was not being seen by Flutus, he started applying medicine to his wounds, and then one of his eyes fell on the wound of Samuel's leg and his wound started to heal and the swelling also ended. Flutus was astonished to see this, and he started weeping with joy. His tears continued to fall on Samuel's wound and all his wounds were healed.

When Samuel woke up the next morning, he was in good health. He wondered how all his wounds were healed overnight. Flutus didn't even tell him anything. He again reached near the mountain in enthusiasm and was about to hit the mountain.

"It is very important for a warrior to know his target and to destroy it, balanced power, continuous strike and a right way is very important otherwise you will be destroyed but not your target. You have used your anger and force for so many days but not the right technique. This mountain is very big in appearance, but a skilled warrior can destroy it in a single strike, you can also do it but first align your power, speed, and confidence", Parkus added.

"Ok! Let's forget breaking this mountain for a while and hit me...hit me if you can", Parkus said in a challenging voice.

"What do you think 'Young Boy', you think you can't?", he laughed at Samuel.

Samuel attacked him and he could not even touch Parkus.

Parkus stopped his every blow with his strong hands very easily. Samuel started hitting him with even more agility and power, but he kept his defense with ease. Then Parkus hit him with a hard punch, and he fell away flying.

Purva, Flutus, Vashi, and all the soldiers and men started gathering at the training site and watching the competition going on between them. Though he fell, everyone was amazed to see his speed and power probably they had not seen anyone like his before.

"How did I beat you?", asked Parkus.

"You are too fast, sharp, and powerful than me", Samuel answered with a gasp.

Prakus smiled and said, "Oh really! I am older and weaker than you. And, even if I am how does it matter to you? I am your target which you must destroy no matter how powerful, skilled, or difficult I am."

"If you feel that your opponent is better than you, my boy.... you have already lost it", Parkus added.

"Do you believe that me being stronger and faster has anything to do with your power, technique, and speed?", Parkus further added.

"Come on...get up and show me the real warrior in you", he said challenging Samuel.

He stood up, took a deep breath, sped towards Parkus, and began hitting him. This time his strikes were very deadly, he couldn't stand before his speed. With a sharp punch from Samuel, he fell away. The fight has begun to be aggressive and deadly. It was difficult to control Samuel. Seeing Parkus beating, his soldiers came to his support and attacked Samuel, but no one could not even touch him, and he defeated them all.

It was not the end yet, Samuel ran towards the mountain at massive speed and, in flight, made a fatal blow at it with his kick at its center. The mountain collapsed in seconds.

Whoever said this, was stunned by Samuel's bravery and strength and began to applaud with joy. Samuel went up to Parkus and touched his feet.

Parkus was overjoyed and he hugged him.

Samuel's training was now at an end. Parkus taught him yoga for mental stability and good health, bow lore, and the art of wrestling war.

Purva was very impressed by Samuel's strength and might. The two often practiced sword fighting together. They both were attracted to each other but never revealed it.

Now it was time for the competition. Parkus called Samuel.

"Sit down", he said. Samuel sat next to him.

You have to leave tomorrow morning to attend the competition. We have registered your name on the bodyguard competition list. Tomorrow at 2 pm the gates of the city will open. You must reach there well before time.

Parkus, extending his hand, gave Samuel folded cloth. It the impression of a Lion's face on it with black and red color also a number was mentioned on it.

"What is it?", asked Samuel.

"This is your identity proof to enter the city. Remember your name is 'Lucifer' but not Samuel. You come from a potter's family, and you have been staying in 'Thajavour' since birth and your father's name is 'Parkus'. This is your identity till you defeat 'Kalazi' and come back", he told Samuel.

Samuel shook his head in consent.

"Now listen to me very carefully", Parkus said.

"Kalazi is an as powerful and equally clever warrior. He has made enough arrangements for his security and kills his enemy even if he gets defeated or killed. No one can go near him unless he wants to. First, you will compete with his giant warriors and dangerous animals. I do not doubt that you will kill them all but remember before you are declared victorious you have to deftly challenge him for the competition. It should not look as if you intend to kill him. If this happens then he will not come to fight with you. You have to say something that hurts his self-esteem, and he will accept your challenge", Parkus added.

"Now two very important things. First, Kalazi wears a sandalwood garland around her neck which holds a small glass vial. That garland is stuck on his body from behind. After killing him, you must remove that garland from his neck safely. Remember, the garland should not be broken, and neither should its glass vessel. Through this rosary, he has subdued all the divine and black powers. If it breaks, the forces emanating from it will kill all those who are there. Kalazi has associated this garland with hir heartbeat with his magical powers. Even if an enemy kills him and the moment his heart stops, there will be a massive explosion in the glass vessel of that garland, and all will be finished."

"Which means I can't kill him?", asked Samuel.

"Yes, and it will not be possible for you to come out of his castle safely after you defeat him because everyone will be after you", Parkus said.

"You told me that I needed to understand two very important things, what is the other one?", Samuel asked.

"Kalazi has a bow. The specialty of this bow is that it can be struck far away from it and the target is sure to be destroyed. No one else is allowed to touch it except him inside the fort. It is heard that if this happens, then in about seven minutes everything inside the fort will be turned to stone. Kalazi always keeps the bow near his throne. If this is true and if we can get that bow, you can come back safely from the fort. And I know who can do this with perfections", Parkus said.

"Who?", asked Samuel.

"It's Purva. She is quick, well trained and an impressive warrior", Parkus replied.

It was evening, Parkus was sharpening his sword at the training site. He called Purva and pointed his sword towards her and said, "It's time to fulfill your duties. You need to play your role for the justice of your mother and family members. Markooz must see his fate and 'Kalazi' is our first step towards the same. Your role will be important, essential, and critical. Undoubtedly, Samuel is a brave boy and has the potential of ruling this country as a king in the future. Everyone needs a companion who holds him in a difficult time, encourages him when defeated, challenges him to achieve more, and doesn't let him deviate from his goal. "

"A woman is his greatest blessing to a man and for Samuel, it is you. I know you like him but now only support him to achieve his goal", Parkus said.

He told her the complete plan and asked her to go along with Samuel to the competition.

The next early morning Samuel got ready and was going towards the stables when Parkus interrupted from behind and said, "You may go to the competition with your old horse and not with your new horse Thunder. I told you, you have to hide your identity until you defeat Kalazi."

Samuel looked back and saw Parkus and Purva standing. He understood that she too would go with him as per the plan.

"I want to take Flutus with me too if you permit", said Samuel.

"If you are sure that you will not get into any trouble because of him, then I do not mind", Parkus said.

Flutus too had arrived by then. Samuel looking at him said, "Flutus is the one who has brought me out of every trouble so far."

Seeing Samuel's faith, tears welled up in his eyes and he embraced Samuel.

"Of course, but the appearance of Flutus is extraordinary, seeing this, the city guards will be suspicious", Parkus said.

"I too have inherited some magical power. Rest assured that no one will recognize me Parkus", Flutus said.

They all took blessings from Parkus and left.

Moving at high speed, he soon reached the main gate of the town. There was a very strong, huge, and heavy door, outside which stood fierce-looking guards of huge stature. There was a long line to go inside the town. All three of them also got in line. Some soldiers were carefully checking everyone's certificates and slowly sending them inside.

Then there was the shouting of the soldiers in anger and a soldier attacked a man and beheaded him. He shouted, "Who else is standing in line with the fake identity? He will have the same fate. Here the punishment for cheating is only death."

Seeing this, many people ran away in fear. The guards were now even more alert. One of them ordered the soldiers "Frisk everyone properly, no one is allowed to take any kind of weapon inside".

All three of them stood calmly and started moving forward. Now it was their turn. A soldier was staring at all three of them. Samuel said in a low voice, "Don't pay attention to him and keep moving forward". After getting their identity checked and frisked, now they had come inside the town.

It was an unbelievable sight for them. "Such a beautiful city!", said the former in astonishment.

It was a beautiful city. There was greenery all around, beautifully built houses, and the aroma of delicious food was coming from every side. One thing to note was that there was a big mirror outside every house. While walking, he came to a crossroads, there was a huge and very tall idol, and everyone was paying obeisance to that idol. They were looking at the idol carefully, when a voice came, 'what are you looking at? bow down, this is the statue of our Kalazi'. It was an old man instructing them.

Without hesitation, they saluted and started moving forward. They noticed that the man was following them. They kept moving and deliberately didn't react. Eventually, that old man was continuously following them. Samuel suggested not to react and keep moving but Purva went to him aggressively and asked him the reason for the same. The old man ran in fear, saying "You will know when you cannot go back!". She ignored but it clicked in Samuel's mind. He asked Flutus to follow him secretly.

Now the most awaited place has come to Fort where the competition was held. One man came at the door and announced.

"My name is Gaba, and I am the chief general of this province. Welcome, all of you. The competition will start from tomorrow morning, you all are given one last chance, if still, no one wants to participate in this competition then you can go back till tonight. Today, after sunset, the main gate to the province will be closed and no one can go out after that. The one who won will remain like this for the rest of his life and the one who loses will leave this world and go away."

"Delicious food, wine, and cultural programs have been organized for all of you. Enjoy life today, don't know if tomorrow", and he started laughing out loud.

It was evening now. Samuel, Purva, and Flutus were taking over the city and making plans for tomorrow's battle. Now the only wait was for tomorrow morning. They were sitting in a dark corner watching everyone. While talking, they fell asleep.

The crucial day had arrived, the bright sun shining brightly across the sky. At the entrance of the fort, the drums started playing loudly and all the warriors started entering inside. All the people of the city were also coming to enjoy the competition.

A soldier stopped Purva and Flutus and said "Your name is not in the ranks of warriors. You can't go to the battlefield. Go and sit in the audience." Samuel pointed and he started walking quietly to the other side.

Now everyone had come inside the fort. There was a lot of enthusiasm in the audience, and they were shouting and applauding. Purva and Flutus had also come and sat there.

All the warriors had arrived on the battlefield. It was a big ground in the middle of the fort, around which the spectators were sitting and the throne of 'Kalazi' was made at a great height in front. All possible dangerous weapons like swords, axes, big hammers, and spears were kept in the middle of the field.

Kalazi enters the battlefield with his bodyguards and soldiers. Samuel was disappointed to see him because he imagined him as very strong, tough-built, and deadly looks. But he appeared to be ordinary. But he was wearing a strong Armor, inside which he had hidden the garland. His bodyguards surrounded him from all sides. He went ahead and sat on his throne. He raised his bow and released an arrow towards the sky. Within a few seconds, a white-colored pigeon falls on the battlefield. The arrow fired by Kalazi was through his body.

Kalazi smiled and said, "Start the competition, he who is weak will fall like this dove and those who are strong will find my favor."

The conch shell sounded, and the competition began. First, the competition for recruitment in the army started. All the warriors started displaying their skills and strength. Some faced the dreaded lion, while some faced the dangerous warriors. Corpses began to fall, and the battlefield turned red with blood.

The victorious warriors were rewarded and recruited into the army and the dead bodies of the defeated warriors were thrown outside the province. There was an atmosphere of panic everywhere. The competition was there earlier also but this time it was very fierce. But seeing so much blood and dead bodies, Kalazi was having a lot of fun.

The next phase of the competition began. Five other warriors were standing with Samuel unarmed on the battlefield. Giant monster warriors attacked them. They were huge and had dangerous weapons. They started inflicting deadly blows on all of them. Samuel continued to deftly defend himself. But the rest of the warriors were not able to face them. One by one those demons started killing the warriors. Someone's neck was separated from the torso and someone's body was ripped into two pieces.

Now Samuel was only left and bravely facing them all. A demon hit him hard, and he fell away. Kalazi said excitedly, "Cut him into pieces too, he doesn't deserve to be my bodyguard." Seeing this whole audience started to cheer.

But Samuel had not even started to fight, and he stood. A warrior came running towards him to attack him; he inflicted a severe blow on his neck with his leg. The warrior fell to the ground and died. A deep silence surrounded the ground, now one must have expected this. All eyes were on him. He moved forward, picked up the sword, and attacked the rest of the giant warriors. One by one they were falling to the ground, a single blow from Samuel was sufficient to kill them. Someone's neck separated from the torso and for a few crossed his sword into their body. He hit the neck of one last warrior so hard that his neck was cut and fell at the feet of Kalazi.

Kalazi stood upon his throne in panic and asked his bodyguards to take him captive. But none of the bodyguards stepped forward. Everyone was surprised to see this. Samuel and Purva too didn't think so either.

"I won your competition, Kalazi, instead of rewarding me, you ordered to keep me captive. 'This is not possible, I challenge you to fight. You said I don't deserve to be your bodyguard. Now you prove, are you even a warrior? Every year to get so many competent and powerful soldiers killed just for the sake of your safety and speak your fear", Samuel said.

"Who...who... are you?", Kalazi asked in a nervous voice. "No ordinary man can kill my people. You are different. An ordinary person cannot kill such powerful warriors of mine and that too in just one blow. Don't hurt me, please", and began to laugh out loud. He raised his sword and put to death all the bodyguards standing beside him for disobeying him.

Kalazi jumped from his throne into the field and stood before Samuel.

"What do you think, I got scared? Kalazi is a lion that chews even the bones of its prey. You are challenging in my province and castle. You came with your wish but will not go back alive", he said to Samuel growling.

"Kid...pick up the weapon of your choice and hit me if you can but I wonder whom all will you hit because I'm not the only one", he started laughing even louder.

Samuel was astonished that ten others exactly like him had appeared in the field, threatening him for battle and laughing out loud.

They all attacked him, and he started to fight with utmost bravery. He understood that this is some illusion of Kalazi but was unable to identify the real one. He only began defending himself because he was afraid that he might not damage the garland around the neck of the real one with his strong blow. Their attack was now getting more and more deadly.

Flutus was upset and worried seeing all this. He was well aware to break such illusions. He quickly ran towards Samuel.

Samuel had fallen on his conscience. And all of them were proceeding to attack him.

"How can a sinner hide his sins, cleanse the body but never wash away the filth of the mind", said Flutus to Samuel.

Flutus picked up a handful of earthenware from the field and blew it towards them all and said to Samuel "The one who has the soil on his clothes is the real one, everything else is a hoax."

Samuel understood that the one who is standing in the fourth place is the real Kalazi. He got up, picked up his sword, and ran towards him. His sword crossed Kalazi's body and he lifted him into the air.

Seeing the end of Kalazi, there was a stampede among the people, and his army began to attack both Samuel and Flutus.

Samuel cried out, "Purva, now!"

Purva ran towards Kalazi's throne at high speed and lifted his bow. As soon as the bow was raised, there was a bolt of loud lightning and a storm started coming.

On the other hand, Samuel had so far taken out the garland by making an incision in Kalazi's neck, he was in much pain but still alive.

All three of them ran towards the gate of the fort. Kalazi's army and bodyguards were chasing them. Whoever came before him, Samuel and Purva would cut them off with their swords and those who were behind had turned to stone. Now they had very little time left to get out of the fort, but the guards closed the gate of the fort, and they could not come out.

They didn't understand anything. Everything was quickly turning to stone.

Samuel saw the same big man. He ran to him and said, "Can you please help us get out?"

The man smiled and said, "Of course". He was none other than Samuel's horse Thunder whom Parkus had sent in disguise. He flew all of them out of the fort. In no time everything inside was converted to stone and even the fort's door.

They all landed safely out of the fort. All the people were standing in the group and were staring at them. They were speechless and scared. Parkus has also reached there by then.

"We are not here to rule you", Samuel said. "You don't have to be afraid of anyone, now you are all safe. Kalazi was a cruel king who to date exploited you only for his benefit. All of you were imprisoned. Now all of you are free, you can lead a good life as per your wish from now."

"Let me introduce you all to your friend Mr. Parkus. He would help you for this new beginning and will support you as and when required", Samuel added.

Everyone started clapping in joy and was happy.

Parkus congratulated Samuel on this win.

The very same evening, Samuel and Purva were sitting together. He was telling her about the struggle and goals of his life. She was listening and looking at him very carefully and her eyes were moist.

"Hey, what happened to you?", Samuel asked and hugged her.

She smiled, came closer to him, and kissed his lips.

"I am with you in all your struggles for a lifetime", she said and sat beside him with her head on his shoulder.

Chapter 5: The Flutus

"Wwhy are you standing here alone? How long have I been looking for you?", asked Samuel.

He looked back, there were tears in his eyes. "I just wanted to be alone", replied Flutus.

"Hey...What happened, is everything ok? Why do you look so sad? I was looking for you to say a big thank you for everything you are and have done for me. If you didn't help me at the right time, it would have been difficult to defeat Kalazi. You helped me once again without caring about your life. Thank you, my friend", Samuel said.

"You are like my brother. I will always help you and protect you", Flutus replied with a smile.

"Oh...that's so sweet. Yes! you are right we are not my friend but a brother from now on", Samuel said hugging him.

"Can I ask you something?", Samuel said.

"Yeah, please", Flutus replied.

"I want to listen to you, want to know about you. I hardly know anything about you except that there is a wonderful man who always comes to my rescue whenever I am in a trouble", Samuel said.

"I want to know my Friend, my brother", he added.

"It is not sufficient what you already know?", Flutus replied.

"Hey, please don't feel bad, it's okay if you are not comfortable. It doesn't matter, that's enough for me to have a good and true friend like you. In whom I trust more than myself. Let's go and have food then we have to leave for Thanjavur also", Samuel said.

Flutus looked at him and asked him to sit next to him and started talking about him.

"Not very far away from Thanjavur, there is a kingdom Kuntal on the high mountains touching the sky. Once upon a time, it was a very powerful, capable, and self-sufficient state. It had a friendship with all the surrounding states and was always taken up in the highest esteem. The specialty of that state was its army, smallest yet deadly and highly skillful. Defeating it in the war was like a dream."

"The second reason for the popularity of state was her princess 'Lipika'. Highly beautiful, intelligent, sharp, and well skilled in archery and swordsmanship. She was the great worrier and backbone of her army. Many prominent warriors had kneeled before her on the battlefield. Under her leadership, the state had reached greater heights and development. "

"I am the only son of princess Lipika", Flutus said.

Samuel looked at him majestically and said, "That's great so I'm talking to a prince."

"I wish it were true, I wish my mother Lipika could remain a princess. But it's not like that, I'm just a curse. For which my mother and I are suffering, and I cannot do anything", said Flutus.

"A happy state like Kuntal was eclipsed by a greedy, cruel and lustful demon. He invaded the kingdom several times but never won. In front of the might of Kuntal's army, he and his army could never even reach close to the border of the state. He was repulsed every time he attacked."

"One day, he encountered Princess Lipka on the battlefield and was defeated very badly. The princess had left him dead. The battle was defeated but at the same time, he was fascinated by the beauty and valor of Princess Lipika. He sent a marriage proposal to the princess, but it was turned down. He knew that it was not possible to conquer Kuntal and Princess Lipika, so he used deceit."

"One night, with the help of his magical knowledge, he entered the invisible palace and fraudulently committed a huge massacre. By the time Princess Lipika could recognize him, he had killed both of her brothers and taken their father captive. He put this condition in front of her that he would not kill her father if she would put Kuntal's army under him and marry him. She was compelled and she surrendered to him. In this way, he subjugated the kingdom of Kuntal and became the king. But he kept her father in his captivity and threatened that he would kill him if she ever tried to go against him."

"Time passed and so did his torture. A happy and prosperous state was now on the verge of destruction. People were sad, upset, and insecure. There was an atmosphere of chaos everywhere. Many times, people used to come to princess Lipika with their requests, but it was of no use. Whoever came with his complaint, he would destroy their family and home and make their women the victims of his lust. Not only this, he and his army men used to rob the respect of any passing girl. Due to fear, either person did not say anything else were killed."

"Seeing this plight of her state and people, she started kneeling inside, she started feeling sad. His health often started deteriorating. One day she came to know that she was pregnant. Maybe after all these years, there was finally the good news for her. She was happy as if she had found a hope to live. "

"She thought that hearing this news my father would be happy and would become a better person, but it did not happen. He pretended as if he didn't care. Time passed and my mother eagerly waited for my birth, but my father was now absorbed in debauchery."

"The time of my mother's pregnancy had passed but I was not born. Seeing this my mother was very stressed and worried. All the doctors were surprised to see why I was not being born despite the completion of time. Fifteen months later I was born, everyone was surprised because to date this has never happened, and no one has heard."

"Seeing my ugly and weak body, the midwife was also scared and was trembling with fear. When my mother saw me for the first time, she was shocked too, but a mother is a mother. She hugged me and started taking care of me. She cried a lot that night, hugging me like her chest. I still feel his pain in my heart."

"Seeing my appearance, my father despised me. One day my father came to my mother and blamed her for my ugly looks and weak body because she never accepted him as her husband else, I would have been as strong as him and told her what his grandmother told him about keeping a relationship with a woman. My mother said that she feels disgusting even with the thought of he is being her husband. He can only claim his forceful right only on her body but can never win her heart."

"Hearing this, he got very angry and tried to kill me. That day she once again raised her sword and once again he could not win. She told him that in a fraction of seconds she can sever his neck from his body, but she is helpless because of her son and father. For my safety, she decided to leave the palace and took me from there."

"The more extraordinary I looked, the more extraordinary I grew. Within one year of my birth, I have become as big as I am today. As time passed, I came to know that I have many magical powers. Maybe I got it from my father. My mother was happy to know this but was equally worried that I might not start misusing them or become like my father."

"She decided to educate me and make me a better person but due to my looks, no one agreed to teach me. She decided to do it on her own and blessed me with extreme knowledge and wisdom and I decided to use my powers for helping people or to achieve a goal for the benefit of humanity."

"Whenever my father and his people tortured someone, I started protecting them. I am happy that I have been able to help and protect so many people to date. But I could not wipe my mother's tears and could free her father from my father's captivity. I had only heard about my father's cruelty t but saw it a few years back. Through some spies, I found out about the prison where my mother's father was imprisoned. He was locked in a dungeon which was never open since locked."

"When I went to rescue him, there was only his skeleton, I do not know when and how he had died. My mother still thinks that he is alive, and I do not dare to tell her the truth. Nor do I have enough power to avenge my mother and her father."

Flutus continued to speak, and tears rolled down his eyes. Samuel hugged him and he wept bitterly.

Seeing Flutus' condition and listening to his story, he got very angry, and he said, "You are my friend, my brother and I cannot see your condition. Come with me, we will attack Kuntal now and put an end to that evil and bring justice to your mother."

Flutus looked at him and asked, "Do you want to know what is his name?"

Samuel asked aggressively, "Yes! I want to."

"The king of Kuntal, the husband of my mother, and my father are Markooz!"

Chapter 6: Unite the Power

As suggested by Lionel, Queen Durgashakti reached Kuntal. She had the name Lipika but nothing else she he had to meet her. But how? This was swirling in her mind.

She reached the main gate of the city. The gatekeeper asked, "Where do you want to go? What do you want? Show me your identity card".

"I wish to go to the palace; I have come in search of a job. I have heard that King's servants are being appointed. So thought maybe my luck may also shine. See this is my identity proof", replied Dugashakti.

Hearing this, the gatekeeper laughed out loud and said, 'Oh...Such a wonderful name 'Chandrika' but poor you, you look old, your youth is over. Go...go, the king's servants must be young, not old women like you", he laughed even louder. "They will through you out of the palace. It is better that you go back yourself from here."

"Please let me go, brother. You are right but let me give it a try. If not the same maybe I get some other work to arrange for my living."

On much insistence, he allowed her to go. She reached the palace and told the soldier standing at the door that she had come to the palace for a job. She was made to meet Paloma.

Paloma was the chief of staff at the palace and a transgender but deep routed and very closed to the queen Ramola (second wife of Markooz).

"Yes...what do you want?", asked Paloma rudely.

"I...I am looking for a job in the palace, please help me out", said Chandrika.

"Get lost, there are no jobs here. Who told you? Just vanish from her before I ask soldiers to though you out", Paloma replied.

"Oh...am sorry but all the way I was coming towards the palace, everyone insisted me to meet the dynamic and kindhearted Paloma. This soldier is such a fool, he made me meet you rather than her. My mistake, I thought of you as Paloma but no worries I will find her and request her excellency to help me out. I have heard so much good about her and I am sure she will help me as she is too good a person and so kind. I wish you could learn something from her rather than being so rude", said Chandrika.

"Hey stop! I am the only one Paloma but tell me, do people talk so highly of me?", she said smiling.

"Of course, her excellency! Oh...I am so glad to meet you. You are the same I thought of, young, beautiful, dynamic, and full of life", Chandrika replied.

"So sweet of you", Paloma said blushing.

"Hmm...you have come to the right person. I always do good to people and will help you too", Paloma added.

"What can you do?", she asked.

"I cook wonderful food", Chandrika replied excitingly.

"See, Queen Ramola is very rigid about keeping people in the palace, but one chance can be given to you". Paloma said.

"You make dinner tonight and if you can make a good impression out of your taste, then your job is confirmed", she added.

Chandrika prepared very tasty food, and everyone started licking their fingers. The praise of Queen Ramola was not stopping. She asked Paloma if she has hired a new cook.

"A woman had come to ask for a job and I allowed her to showcase her talent'. With your permission can she be hired", Paloma asked.

Chandrika got a job as a cook and started working there. About a month passed and one day, Pamola said, "Take this, today's menu. Have a look at it properly and remember today's dinner is very special. So, make great food", Paloma said.

"Looking at the list", Chandrika said, "What is so special today?"

"Hey! Today King's son is coming for the meal and King Markooz himself will be joining for the dinner. You only need to do all the preparations for today and these people will be assisting you. Get well dressed, today you are going to meet people from the royal family for the first time. Also, I will be much busy in the preparation, see you in the evening", she smiled and left.

Chandrika was surprised how come the king of Kuntal was Markooz. Her anger knew no bounds when she heard his name. She controlled herself and started cooking. She was now eagerly waiting for the night. Because whose name she had heard till today, will be in front of her today.

It was evening, Chandrika reached the palace and started arranging dinner in a large Hall. There were big pictures all around on the walls of that hall. She asked a soldier standing there, 'Whose pictures are these?'.

Looks like a new one has come here, said the soldier. The biggest picture in the center of the wall is that of our king Markooz, his left queen Ramola and right side his son Zain who is the present king of Mazar. He is the one coming for dinner today.

"Mazar, where is it? Till today the name has not even been heard", said Chandrika in surprise.

"If you have not heard that doesn't mean it doesn't exist. It is one of the biggest states, was early know as 'Thanjavur' which is now renamed as 'Mazar' after King Markooz defeated that state in war", the soldier replied.

"Hmm....and what are those pictures on the other wall?", she asked.

"Oh, that's not important though. The lady that you see is 'Lipika' the first wife of king Markooz and the ugly and rare child seen in her lap is her son 'Flutus'."

"Many years ago, she left the palace with her son", he added.

Chandrika curiously asked, 'Where is she now?'.

"Well, she is alive at the mercy of the king and lives in the big temple of the city. No one is allowed to visit there except the king. And if you love your life, don't even take her name in front of anyone in the palace", said the soldier.

"But why so?", Chandrika asked.

"Lipika was the princess of this state and highly beautiful. Though she doesn't live here, the king still loves her and this makes Queen Ramola jealous. It is just that she is not able to get her kissed out of king's fear", the soldier whispered.

"Come here, let me show you, said the soldier and took her to the big window of that hall and from afar showed the temple where Lipika used to live."

"What a wonderful view, from here the whole city is visible", said Chandrika.

"Entire city?", he smiled, "From here all the states around the city are visible. Look at this instrument, you can see far away from it. All the surrounding kingdoms are ruled by King Markooz and from here he keeps an eye on everyone. This is one of the specialties Kuntal, being on the height from where everything is kept track of", the soldier said.

They heard someone's arrival and got to work.

After some time, the guests started arriving. Paloma had also arrived, and she was very happy with the arrangements made by Chandrika. Queen Ramola and her son Zain had also arrived. But Chandrika's eyes were waiting for Markooz.

There was a stir in the room and all eyes were on the door. Mark was coming. He had his bodyguards all around him. A detachment of the army stood around the room for security. Chandrika was looking at him without blinking. She felt like killing him right there.

Zain hugged Markooz and they started to talk. Everyone got busy talking and having food. Chandrika was closely observing everyone, especially Markooz.

"Any news at your end?", asked Markooz to Zain.

"Yes father, a surprising one. Someone has killed 'Kalazi' and has taken over his state", said Zain.

"You must find out and kill him, all states must be under us only. I am surprised how come you are sitting quite by now, Markooz replied in anger.

"No father that is not the case, I am only trying to figure out how can someone do it so easily which we could not do for years. One important thing to note for you is that your dearest son, Flutus, was also seen there. According to our detectives, a boy and a girl were also with him. That boy had participated in the competition", Zain explained.

"This is not a good sign. You must find out at the earliest and kill that boy as soon as possible", Markooz said angrily.

"Please take your food, Zain has come after so many days. All these things can happen later also", Ramola said requesting.

Stress, great concern, and fear was clearly visible on Markooz's face. Seeing this, Chandrika's mind was relieved. At the same time, she was also curious to know who was 'Kalazi' and he got so distraught as he was killed.

After the end of the meal, everyone started leaving. Paloma introduced Chandrika to Queen Ramola. The queen greatly appreciated her food and presented her the precious state coin as a reward and left.

"I am impressed, someone is rarely regarded so high by the Queen Ramola that too so early and all above with this precious royal state coin. This is your gate pass to go anywhere in the state. You are now the part of royal staff members", Paloma complemented Chandrika.

This is what Chandrika was looking for, now her vision was clear, and all her confusion was gone. She was next up on meeting Lipika at the earliest. Leaving the palace without information was risky & creating doubt. The next day she took permission from Paloma for going to the local market to buy some personal stuff.

She reached the temple and somehow managed to get entry inside by showing the State Coin. Lipika was in meditation. She moved towards her but could not move forward except few steps. She felt as if someone was pulling her back. She tried a lot but could not go any further.

"You can't move ahead", said Lipika while opening her eyes.

"Tell me the purpose of your visit, who are you, why have you come here and what do you want from me", she asked.

"I want to visit this temple and don't you think it is not right on you to block the way of people coming inside. Everyone has the right to come to a temple so do I", Chandrika replied.

"I have been staying here for a decade now and not one has come to this temple except you. How should I believe that it's your only purpose?", Lipika said.

"Certainly, your purpose is something else so either you tell the same or go back", she added.

"I have come here to meet someone who gave up everything for his son years ago. Who could achieve everything with the power of her sword but did not? I have come to ask Lipika, why did she choose darkness for herself when she had the capability of being in light always. Why did she choose isolation in this temple? And before you ask me who I am let me tell you myself I am 'Durgashakti', the queen of Thanjavur whose king was brutally killed by your husband Markooz."

They both looked at each other in deep silence for minutes and Lipika replied, "There is no one here whom you call Markooz's wife. Here who lives is a mother, a daughter, and a princess who is seeing the ruin of her state every day and her name is Lipika whom you have come to meet."

"You can move forward now", she said.

Durgashakti moved forward and sat next to Lipika. "I need your help", she said.

"Lionel told me one day you will come looking for me", she replied.

"How come you know him?", Durgashakti asked.

"Who doesn't know him, one of the greatest warriors and now a brilliant teacher? I had gone to him first seeking help to save my state and later requesting him to train my son. He could not train him due to his weak body. From him I came to know about Nirvana, how Markooz cheated him in war and killed him", she said.

"Lionel had said that Markooz is such darkness that will slowly swallow the whole world. It is impossible to put an end to him because of his black powers. Even if he gets defeated on the battlefield, no one can kill him. He has created such a protective shield of his death with his magical powers, without knowing that secret his death is impossible."

"Markooz had only two reasons for his subjugation to Kuntal. First political so that he could stay here and maintain control over all the states under his control. Second, take our powerful army under his control. He was badly defeated every time and in the last war, he got another reason; the reason was me. He was fascinated by me."

"He obtained Kuntal by deceit and constrained me by taking my father captive. I was helpless then but agreeing to marry him was my choice and plan. Markooz can do everything but cannot harm me. I accepted his marriage proposal as suggested by Lionel. This was the only way to know the secret of his death."

"Every day spent with him was like a punishment. I made a choice, but I lost my honor and respect. I kept silently watching the atrocities committed on my people. I could put him to death whenever I wanted. He knows nothing but deceit and deceit. I did the same thing, I killed my soul and made him believe that I love him too and remained weak because I knew my goal."

"When my goal was achieved, I left from there with my son. My own people have different thoughts about me, some feel that I did this to save my father, and some feel for my son and left them alone to face the tragedy. But I did all this to get Markooz to reach his bowels. I compromised on myself to give them a good life which they always had. I did all that a princess should do for her people. I was neither weak then nor am I weak today, but not every battle is fought on the battlefield. My fight with Markooz has been going on for years and it will either end with him or mine", Lipika kept on talking and tears flowed from her eyes.

"Is your father still under his custody?", Durgashakti asked.

"No, he died within a few months after he was put in the dungeon", Lipika replied.

"And did you find out the secret of his death", Durgashakti asked.

"Yes, I did", Lipika replied.

"Now it's time to leave from here. Lionel had said that after meeting you, both of us should come to his place. But if I disappear from here, Markooz will try his best to find me and his spies may also come to Lionel's monastery. His guards keep a constant watch on this temple for my safety and security but no one is allowed to come inside. How did you enter the temple? Did the guards not stop you?", Lipika said.

"They did actually, but I had shown them the royal coin and said King Markooz have sent food for you with your permission", Durgashakti replied.

"Do they know your name too?", Lipika asked.

"Yes, but not the real one. Everyone knows me here as Chandrika but not Durgashakti", she said.

"Then what is the plan?", Durgashakti asked

"We will beat him in his way, 'Magic'", Lipika said.

"But how?", she asked.

"By creating an illusion, we need a dead body which will be made my lookalike through magic", Lipika said.

"But how this is possible and who will do that?", she asked in surprise.

"It is possible and I will do it", a voice said. Durgashakti looked back. Flutus was standing behind her.

Before she could say anything, Lipika replied, "He is my son Flutus. He has got magical powers from birth."

Flutus bowed to Durgashakti and hugged Lipika, crying he said, "You knew mother your father was dead. You have sacrificed a lot in your life, now it is the turn of justice."

"I must go back to the palace now else people may doubt", Durgashakti said.

"Yes, you should go now. We will meet tomorrow before sunset at the main gate of the city", said Lipika.

When Durgashakti was going back to the palace, she realized that someone was following her. She tried many times but could not find out.

The next day while she was cooking food when someone put a sword on her neck and asked, "Now tell your truth". She looked back, that was 'Paloma'.

"Where were you yesterday? Certainly not in the market."

"Why did you go to the temple? Do you know the Lipika? Did you go there to meet her? You thought you will fool me with your smooth talk? I understood something is fishy on the very first day you had come here. I only requested Queen Ramola to appoint you as a cook. At my behest, that soldier was keeping an eye on you and was eagerly answering all your answers. Last night too you had all eyes on what everyone is doing and talking", Paloma said with a cunning smile.

"Now you have two ways", said Ramola as she entered the kitchen. "Get ready to be killed or kill her which should look like a perfect accident. In return, we will get you out of the city safely. But if you do any trick then remember, along with Lipika, your death will also remain an accident."

"What are you thinking, answer quickly", Paloma said, raising the sword towards her.

This was happening contrary to what Durgashakti had imagined. But she kept her patience and said "Yes" to kill Lipika.

"Good choice but how will you do this?", asked Ramola.

"I will go to meet Lipika again in the temple and I will kill her and set her body and the whole temple on fire so that it will look like it was an accident, and everything will be burnt to ashes. And no one will ever know the truth", she said.

"Sounds good, Paloma, and this soldier will be coming with you. Now you can leave do the needful. Today must be the last sunset of Lipika." she said.

Ramola whispered in Paloma's ear, "Kill her and burn her with Lipika in the temple."

They all left for the temple. The soldier entered the temple through a secret passage, and both went inside the temple through the main gate. Lipika was surprised to see her and asked, "You are here again and that too now?" and she noticed Paloma standing behind her with a sword in her hand. She understood that something is wrong or maybe they have come to know about the reality of Chandrika. She asked consciously, "Why have you come here?".

"Chandrika, take this sword and end it by slitting her throat", said Paloma.

Chandrika turned to Lipika and said, "Today is the sunset of someone's life, do you know whose? Not you but her". She turned around quickly and with a loud shout slit Paloma's throat. Blood started pouring down Paloma's throat and she died within a stick. Seeing this, the soldier attacked her, and she also killed that soldier.

Dugashakti narrated the incident that took place in the palace and according. They set the temple on fire from all sides, and both left safely with Flutes.

Markooz was very surprised to hear the news of Lipika's death. Ramola tried to convince him that she had died in the temple accident, but he did not believe it.

His havoc wreaked on the security guards of the temple and all of them were mercilessly slaughtered. No one had seen this side of Marzooz before.

He was stunned to hear the news of Lipika's death, but he believed that she could never die like this as she was a skilled and cunning warrior. He understood that it was a conspiracy and wanted to find out as soon as possible at any cost. He asked his trusted general, Haliba, to trace all the developments. From the investigation of the burnt bodies found in the temple, it was also found that none of them is the dead body of Lipika, that is, she was alive.

Meanwhile, Durgashakti, Lipika, and Flutus had reached Lionel's ashram. Samuel, Parkus, and the East had also come.

After the meal, Lionel and the rest others went to Fiona's hut. She was sitting unconscious.

"Who is she and what are these pictures on the wall?", Samuel asked.

"It is a description of the desire of the heart and the eyes of a hapless mother. Her name is Fiona and this is your grandmother Samuel", said Lionel. Samuel looked at her with curiosity and wonder, but he didn't say anything.

Samuel asked again, "What do these pictures mean and why is it not saying anything?"

"The scene on this side of the wall shows how his brave son got killed by deceit. And the picture on the other side is her wish which she has been waiting for so long to be fulfilled. Do you know who this small boy in this picture is?", Lionel asked.

"It's you", he added.

"Now is the right time, we must give justice to our people. Our goal is before us, and we all must unite and support each other and achieve what we all have been waiting for. We must fight and destroy a power whose stature has tremendously increased with each passing year", Lionel further added.

"Parkus and I have closely approximated Markooz's growing powers and army strength. He presently has the support of more than thirty states who will fight from his side if not by choice but out of fear. He has a military headcount of over two lakhs and especially the control over the unbeaten army of Kuntal", Lionel said.

"Markooz's existence is not his military power but his magical powers. He is not a warrior but a killer who dazzles his opponent only by deceit", Fiona said.

Everyone surprisingly looked at her as she had hardly spoken anything for years.

"I am proud of my son Nirvana, who stood alone for saving his people and the pride of the nation. Of course, he was killed that day, but Markooz and his army had his fear all the time. The fear was so much that when my son got injured and fell to the ground, none of them dared to even come near him. In front of my eyes, I saw his demons and soul's army sucking his blood. He was slowly lying in the lap of death, I tried to save him but there was such a trap around him that it was difficult to reach him. He fought till the last drop of his blood", she said.

"He made Markooz seriously injured and almost dead, but he still didn't die, surely there is some secret to his death that we must find out. History is witness that he has not won any war on the strength of his ability and army only with the help of deceit and his magic powers. His nature is to only cheat." She added

She came to Samuel with staggering steps and said, "My son and your father have lost their lives to save their people. Can you do justice to everyone by performing the duty of a prince?", she said.

Samuel hugged her with tears in his eyes. "Hold your tears, Samuel. I have not let mine come out. Now it will flow only in tribute to my son after Markooz reaches his end", she said.

Durgashakti hugged Fiona and said, "I can understand your pain. A mother has seen her son and a wife has seen her husband die before their very eyes. We have seen our prosperous and happy state getting destroyed and my people being forced to migrate. Now such a storm of vengeance will arise in which Markooz and his everything will be destroyed."

"We are grateful that you are with us in this war and struggle", Lionel said to Lipika.

"In this war, we are all fighting our own personal battle in which our enemy is the same. All of us have lived our lives in utter darkness because of this one person", Lipika said.

She came close to Fiona held her hand and said, "You are right, even after defeating him on the battlefield, he will not die. Even if a single drop of blood is taken out of his body, he would not die. Even if countless arrows pierce his body, he will not die because his life is in his four-headed horse".

"So, we just need to kill his horse, it will be all over", Parkus said excitedly.

"It can't be simple. He is a clever and maneuverable warrior. If he has secured his death, it certainly wouldn't be that easy", said Samuel.

"Do we have any further information on this?", Samuel asked Lipika.

"As far as I know, he has hidden his heart in the neck of his four-headed horse. Any and every kind of weapon made of metal, wood, or stone can injure Markooz and his horse but cannot kill them. But as soon as his heart stops beating, both himself and his horse will die. And how it will happen, this secret is either known to him or his maternal grandmother 'Aulika' to whom he killed himself", Lipika said.

"Difficult but not impossible. Get ready for your one more journey, Samuel", Lionel said.

"If he cannot die from a weapon made of metal, stone, wood, then one thing can definitely be of our use", he added.

"What?", Samuel looked at him curiously.

"Crystal, a solid material whose constituents are arranged in a highly ordered microscopic structure, forming a crystal lattice that extends in all directions. They are solid and sharp and can easily pierce a base", Lionel explained.

"And where do we find them?", Samuel asked.

"We not only need to find but must get the best one. It is heard that towards the west direction from here after crossing the vast ocean and dangerous deserts, there is a valley known as 'Crystal Valley' between the flying mountains next to 'Redoubt Volcano'. The flowing lava of that volcano keeps falling on the crystals located there and makes them strong and deadly", Lionel said.

"This journey will be very much different and dangerous from all the rest. The challenges will be huge as ever and they will have to be faced with great tact and caution. I don't have any other information about that place but surely believe that you have the capability to reach there and achieve your goal", Lionel explained to Samuel.

"I'm ready", said Samuel.

"Not only you, we", Flutus and Purva also said.

"We are also coming with you because you will need us. You can surely achieve anything alone, but we will multiple your strength", said Purva smiling.

"That's better, I too suggest the same. Prepare to leave, I pray to God that all of you will be victorious in your goal and return soon", Lionel said.

It was evening time. Everyone was resting after dinner.

Samuel was preparing for his journey. Tightening the reins of his horse Thunder. He said, "You will play a big role in this journey, I am thankful that you chose me."

"Thank you, Samuel". He turned back. Flutus was standing behind him.

"Why are you thanking me?", said Samuel.

"Because even after knowing my truth, you didn't give up on me", said Flutus.

"Your truth is that you are a kindhearted, brave, and good person and my only friend. It was your destiny to be the son of Markooz but you chose to be a better person. Nothing will ever change between us; you will always be my friend", he said hugging Flutus.

The next day Samuel, Flutus, and Purva came to meet everyone before leaving for Crystal Valley.

"Surely your amazing horse 'Thunder' can fly high in the sky, but I suggest using it only when necessary so that he doesn't get tired. You don't know about the path forward before you. First a vast ocean then dense desert but no clarity how challenging this going to be", Parkus said.

Parkus placed a light blue conch on Samuel's hand and said, "It would help you cross the sea. If its color is blue, understand that the way is clear and when it starts turning black, a terrible storm is about to come. Near the sea, you will find many sailors who can make you reach the other side of the ship and reach you on it soon in their ship. Choose them wisely because they will want something from you in return."

They left after seeking everyone's blessing!

Chapter 7: The Crystal Island

A huge sea was before them. It's almost impossible to estimate the depth.

"Do you have a solution 'Flutus' as to how soon we can cross this sea?", asked Samuel.

Samuel and Purva looked at him.

"Why are you guys staring at me like this?", Flutus exclaimed.

"Show me some magic my friend, I need a ship to sail through this sea at the earliest", Samuel said.

Flutus put his hand in the bag hanging over his shoulder and placed a small ark on Samuel's hand.

"What a joke, do you think we would do this on the vast ocean with such a small ship", said Samuel in astonishment.

"Put it in the water and see the magic my friend", Flutus replied.

As soon as Samuel put it in the water, it became a huge ship.

"Wow...amazing...brilliant!", Samuel replied.

"So, who will sail it and take us through?", Samuel asked.

"You asked for only a ship but not a sailor! It was not talked about", Flutus said with a smile.

A drunk man staggeringly approached the ship and said, "Where did it come from? Never seen such a huge ship", he said, scratching his head.

"Is this ship yours, this is so cool", he asked Samuel.

"What do you have to do with this, run away from here", said Samuel rudely.

"No one has ever insulted Captain Moja like this, if my ship is destroyed that does not mean anyone will just misbehave with me", he said angrily.

"Oh my god! What's the pleasure meeting you 'Captain Mojo'", Purva said with a twinkle in her eyes to Samuel. "We are sorry we could not recognize the Captain Great, please forgive us and help us, please."

"You look sensible to me and pretty too. So, tell me lady what can I do for you", he said in a flirting voice.

"Oh Captain, we need to reach the other side of the sea at the earliest. We have such a great ship, but our sailor ditched us at the last moment and ran away. We probably need somebody great and experienced captain like you", she said to him in a flirting voice too.

"Ahm...of course...of course where exactly do you all need to go", asked Captain Mojo.

"We need to head towards the desert so that we can earliest reach, Redoubt Volcano", Purva replied.

Hearing this, he stared at Purva and said, "Are you out of your senses?", he shouted. "No...No...I will not go there."

"It is good that your Sailor ran away, the poor man's life is saved. You all have made a plan to commit suicide and I am out of it. He turned around and said, don't you love your life that you want to go there to get killed?" He started walking away from her in a panic.

Purva followed him and requested a lot, but he did not agree and kept refusing.

He said shouting, "The sea looks calm and beautiful and calm only from outside. As far as you go inside it, you will be trapped in its maze. Listen to me please, drop the of going to the other side. My whole life has been spent in this sea; I know what it is. Just go back!"

"Maybe even if you survive the sea storm, but what will you do with the rain of deadly and hungry fish? What will you do with the flying crocodiles which don't even leave their bones? How will you escape from the rain of fire that consumes everything in a rod?", Captain Mojo said worrying.

"Enough!", said Samuel. "Ok...suppose everything you are saying is 'true', image if you can take us there, survive and come back alive. Wouldn't the stature and status of Captain Mojo be the 'Greatest'!"

"Captain! Death can come anywhere even right here right now but a real man never gets afraid and face all the troubles. The real identity of a person and the capability of his power is realized only in odd circumstances. That's why some people become great and some just pass their life with the help of fear. And that's what you are doing right now", Samuel added.

"I'm sorry Purva, you are wasting your time. If you this Captain Mojo brave and great man, he just proved not to be", Samuel said to Purva.

"And anyway, if whatever he just said is right then I don't think he has the courage of finding out the truth rather than telling us what he has just listened to and confusing. What he is saying is nothing but fake stories but not the truth for sure. But we are not cowards like him, we are going to know the truth and tell the world. Let me him Olive in his illusion, it's his choice. We gave him a choice and chance of being called The Great Captain Moja, ahh...but sad. He actually missed it, neither does anyone know of him today nor will know tomorrow."

"Can you ask this boy to mind his language, he doesn't know anything about me", Captain Moja said angrily to Purva.

"And you don't know me! I have to be there, and I need the help of your experience. And I promise I will not let you happen anything. And remember, what I say I really do", Samuel said to Captain.

After a deep thought, Captain Mojo said, "I do not know what your goal is, for which you are all ready to risk your life. But I am very impressed to see your determination, belief, and faith in each other. I'm in, Captain Mojo at your service!"

They all boarded the ship. The captain took out a compass from his dirty and torn bag and started sailing the ship. In no time they came out from the shore. There were also boats and ships of many fishermen in the sea. Everyone was surprised because no one had ever seen such a huge, modern, and beautiful ship. They had come quite far inside the sea.

Samuel's attention was drawn to the conch shell given by Parkus. It was a matter of surprise that it had turned dark red. Samuel was surprised because Parkus said it would either turn blue or black during a storm. But he could understand something dangerous was above to happen.

"Everyone attention! It has begun, hide and save yourself", said Captain Moja in a terrified voice.

Samuels came running to the deck and what he saw from his telescope was breathtaking. Flying crocodiles were heading towards their ship and they were many in numbers. They had a human-like body but an ugly and scary crocodile face that had sharp long teeth, from whose grip no one can escape. They started landing on the ship deck one by one. Purva fired an arrow from her bow and hit it hard. Pointed arrows pierced their body. The impact was so high that many of them fell into the sea.

Samuel raised his sword and inflicted fatal blows on them, but they started to multiply and it was much more difficult to control them. But he would have come twice as many as he had died. They were now such a large number that it was very difficult to deal with. Flutus built a protective shield around Samuel's horse Thunder to protect him.

Captain Mojo also came to his aid with a sword and said, "It won't stop. If you will kill one, ten more will appear. To kill them, it is necessary to end their source."

"Little away from here there is a long & very high hill. I have heard that their lives 'Dikaso', the king crocodile. This is his army. This all can end only by killing him, otherwise, they will become innumerable and will eat this ship along with us. It is heard that as long as the king crocodile can see, it is impossible to even go near him. If someone breaks both his eyes at once, then only he can be killed by going to him. But the impossible task is to reach the top of that hill", said Captain Mojo.

"You go and kill him, Samuel, I keep them all in a circle so that it can't harm us and the ship. But do it soon because they cannot be stopped for long".

Samuel, without hesitation, took off in the sky with his horse Thunder and reached the top of the mountain with speed. He released the arrow from his bow. It was this perfect aiming bow that he had snatched from Kalazi. The arrow pierced its target across the rod, and he heard a loud sound of groaning in someone's pain. He followed the voice and soon reach there. He was none other than 'Dikaso' the king crocodile. Samuel could recognize him, as he also had a human-like body with a crocodile face. As Samuel moved closer to him, he asked, "Who are you? Is that you who have pierced my eyes? I am in so much pain. What is that you want from me?", he asked.

"Yes, I am the one and I am here to kill you now because unless I do the same. I will not be able to save my people and my ship from your army", Samuel replied.

"Please don't kill me, we will make no harm to you. Please forgive me and in return, I will do want ever you want", he said pleading.

Samuel thought for a while and said, "First, roll back your army from my ship with no damage and hurting any of my people, and secondly I want to know, how they get multiplied as one gets killed."

"We are blessed by the superpower God! It is the result of my extreme penance which I did to save my species", Dikaso said.

"Go on, I am listening", Samuel said with a sarcastic laugh.

"You think it's a joke? I am not lying", Dikaso replied.

"We were never like this, but circumstances have forced us to live this isolated life with so much fear and struggle to survive. We are one of the very rare and unique species left in this world. We can do everything like you humans do but we were never accepted by your society because of our scary bodies and this crocodile face. A long year back we had a wonderful village next to the seashore but were always seen with hatred and were getting killed out of fear. We were living happily with no disturbance to anyone, never hurt anyone, and depended on the sea and nature for our survival. But we often began to attack and got killed, some time out of hatred, fear, and then for the trade of our skin and long precious teeth. We have tremendously begun to reduce the number. Seeing this my father 'Jamelle' started to revolt for saving the rest of us. We are strong but not greedy and dangerous like you humans. We began to get trapped and killed. One day a big attack was made on us wherein I lost my everything, my father, my brother, family but I and few of us could run away and survive."

"For many months we were hidden under the sea. But that life was not acceptable to me. Sitting inside the sea, I did severe penance and one day the deity of the sea appeared. I asked him for a boon to save and protect our species. He said "you are a savior for your species because your tenacity is selfless. As long as there is a single drop of blood left in your body, your species will not end. But you must ensure that you are never hurt because of being in the water for a long time, your body has become very weak. Any wound on your body will never heal and blood will continue to flow from it which will lead to the end of your species. If anyone tries to kill you, it will be consumed before your eyes. And if any other apart from you get killed, every single drop of the blood of his will immediately make a look alike. But You will also be the core, if you died it's all over."

"The god of the ocean disappeared by giving this boon. I was happy but worried about my safety to save everyone. We decided to come to an isolated place and make every effort to stay away from humans and never allowed anyone to come near this place. You are an extraordinarily brave person who could reach this place, but you have given me a wound which will soon end all of us", Dikaso said sobbing.

Listening to him, Samule was extremely sad.

He filled wet soil lying nearby in both his eyes, which reduced the flow of blood but did not stop completely. Dikaso said something in his painful voice. On the other side, all the crocodiles started disappearing from the ship. Flutus understood that Samuel had succeeded.

"Whatever I did, I did it for the safety of myself and my people. Please forgive me", Samuel said to Dikaso.

"No, it's perfectly fine. At least you tried to save me and helped reduce my blood flow. You are the first humans I have known till today who are generous and kindhearted. It would be great if my people and I could be of any help to you, even though only a little time is left for all of us", Dikaso replied.

"Thank you very much for the offer, I am on a mission and would be needing the help of friends like you. I must go now as I have very less time with me to achieve what I want. Please take care", and he left for the ship. Everyone was glad to see him back.

Samuel narrated the entire incident to Captain Mojo, Purva, and Flutus. They began to move forward. The sea was silent and clear.

"It is not a good sign", said Captain Mojo.

"What happened?", Samuel asked.

"This silence is the knock of the coming storm. Get ready, another trouble is on the way", said Captain Mojo.

Samuel looked at the conch and this time it had turned black, which means a storm is on its way. The sky was surrounded by thick dark clouds and lightning started to make a loud noise. His ship got stuck in the high waves of the sea and then a severe cyclone started. The cyclone was so strong that it was very difficult to handle the ship.

Samuel asked Flutus, "Is this ship strong?"

"Hold on firmly and stand, no one can fall out of the ship. As long as we are inside this ship, this storm cannot harm us", Flutus said.

The storm had badly engulfed the ship, and they all were unconscious. After some time, when their eyes opened, they saw themselves in a desert. Their ship was lying a short distance away and was safe. Samuel hurriedly ran towards the ship and looked for his horse Thunder. Fortunately, he was also fine.

They were all astonished at how they reached this desert from the sea. It was very hot, which was difficult to bear.

"How come we are here and what is this desert", Purva asked.

Samuel was watching something very carefully. He replied, "Parkus had said that after the sea, a vast desert will come, perhaps it is the same."

"Do you know anything about this place?", Samuel asked Captain Mojo.

"Not really but we should leave go from here at the earliest as I am not getting very positive vibes from this place. Yes! But I think, the volcano is not very far off from here", Captain Mojo said.

"What are you looking at so carefully, Samuel?", Purva asked.

"I am looking at that road right in the center of this forest and the cone-shaped milestones on both sides", he replied.

"He turned at Flutus and before could say anything", Flutus said, "Ok, Got it."

Flutus chuckled and a chariot appeared in front of him. He tied Thunder to the chariot and asked everyone to ride on it. He was about to move on when -

"One minute", said Flutus and ran towards the ship and as soon as he touched it, it became small again. He put the ship in his bag and rode on the chariot and said, "Let's go now!"

Seeing this, Captain Mojo's mouth was wide open, and he kept looking at Flutus furiously.

They all started moving on that road. There were thorny bushes on both sides. As they moved forward the sight around was getting scary. Samuel has all his focus on the milestones on both say as he could a see the continuous change in their color, not only, signs were continuously appearing and disappearing on the same.

A sudden storm pulls them into a plain area where they find the remains of humans and huge animals, probably the monsters. It was huge ground in the center of sand dunes with bones stacked all over.

The wind was so strong that the chariot could not move forward. The sky had turned so dark as if it were a night in the day. The thunder started cracking loudly. As a Diablos, a horned, subterranean monster, approaches them and attacks their chariot. The attack was so fatal that the chariot collapses. They all fell far away. The Diablos attacks Captain Mojo and he gets severely injured.

At some distance, Purva was lying unconscious. The monster was about to trample her under his feet. Samuel raised his sword, walks up to Diablos, leaped high, and put his sword through his forehead. Samuel grabbed the sword, slid it down, and cut through his mouth and neck. He drops the sword and jumps down, and the monster falls sobbing. With his death, the sky gets clear, and the sun comes out as earlier.

A hunter was hiding behind the bone stacks watching all this and was following all of them since they had come to the desert. Flutus ran towards Captain Mojo. He was badly injured and was moaning in pain. As soon as he put his hands on her wounds, they started to heal, and he was completely fine.

Purva was still unconscious, Samuel shook her vigorously and tried to bring her to her senses. She was breathing very low. His hand touched her waist and he saw that a broken tooth of the monster had entered her waist and it was bleeding. Her body was slowly turning blue, and she was slowly drowning towards her end.

Samuel never thought this would happen nor was ready for it, he cuddled her tightly and said crying expressing his love for the first time, "We're together for a lifetime, you can't leave me like this. I was not even able to tell you, how much I need you and love you. Please come back we have a long way to go!"

Seeing this, Flutus and Captain Mojo ran towards him.

"Samuel, see there!", Flutus shouted.

His horse Thunder had also fallen at some distance, and someone was pulling him very fast towards the sand.

"I'll take care of Purva, you please go and save him", said Flutus.

Samuel raised his bow and left towards Thunder. He was still far away from him. He carefully saw that his body was carried by several dwarf men on their shoulders and was running away with it.

He shouted out loud 'Stop!'. But they started running even harder. Raining arrows with his bow, he erected a wall of arrows in front of them and they could not move forward. He aimed at the and shot an arrow towards them but surprisingly an arrow was shot from the other direction breaking his arrow into pieces. He targeted them again and the same thing happened. It was someone who was protecting those dwarf men.

A hunter who was observing them came before him and said, "It's me and till I am here you can't do any harm to them."

"They are taking away my horse and I will everything to save them", Samuel replied.

"Yes, they are but to save him, not harm and I suggest your other people should also leave that ground immediately and come on the sand, otherwise your bones will only be left till tomorrow morning. The long road and this wide ground that you see is actually a swamp. At the sunset, it becomes a swamp, and everything placed on it gets burnt. They are saving your horse by not intent to cause any harm. Trust me, go and save them first", he said.

It was above sunset, Samuel quickly moved Purva, Flutus, and Captain Mojo from the ground and brought them to the sand.

As Hunter had said, a swamp formed there.

"Thank you!", Samuel said. But he was still worried about Purva not coming to her senses. Flutus also tried a lot but this time even his magic was not working.

A dwarf came to her. He plucked a hair from his long beard, took out the tooth that had entered her waist, and sealed his wound with a needle-like object from his hair. Then he spits on her wound and rubbed it. Purva's health started improving.

Then he moved towards Samuel's horse and pulled his tail vigorously. As soon as he did, Thunder stood up.

All the dwarf men started laughing and slapping, and the hunter too smiled.

Samuel hugged him and thanked him.

"Who are you all and what are you doing in this deserted desert?", Samuel asked.

"I am the caretaker of this desert, and these are my helpers. We are here for over 100 years. Our forefathers have been doing this always. A variety of people come here and make then reach their destination as per their intentions. We get to know the same as soon as a person arrives here. We throw him into this swamp, who has deceit and greed in his mind, but we show him the way forward who comes here for a true and a noble cause. You all are a good-hearted people, and your motive is also noble, that's why we protected all of you." Indicating towards Purva he said, "She will also be fine till morning".

"We must not stay here because it's going to be unbearable cold; you can come to our huts and take some rest", the Hunter said.

Samuel picked up Purva in his lap and they all followed him. Soon they arrived. They had beautiful & highly decorated built huts. After a delicious meal, they all fell asleep.

The next morning, "We need to reach Crystal valley at 'Redoubt Volcano', can you please show us the way?", Samuel asked The Hunter.

"Probably that's what is my job here unless I know your reason to go there", he asked.

"I'm sorry but I can't disclose the reason to you, Samuel (am image of Markooz, his father Nirvana and his life travels through his mind)"

The Hunter Smiled, "I told you I can read minds. The journey forward here is only yours hence your friends can not go ahead. But they can stay safe here till you come back and if you wouldn't I will show them the way back", he replied.

"But...but why can't they come with me?", Samuel asked.

"You need to be there to win over someone's death and that person had secured his death in such a way with his skills, competency, and knowledge. It has to be fair; this is your fight from here which you need to win by proving yourself better than him. Few journeys have to be taken alone; no friend, no family but only you and God!"

"You were able to reach here because of fight intention and a purpose which will change many lives", he said.

"Hmm, got it. Show me the way forward and rest will see", Samuel said confidently.

A dwarf came up to Hunter and said something in his ear. In his hand was a hammer made of stone.

"You'll need it", Hunter pointed at Samuel. "I will lead you to the exit gate of this desert. You have to pass through burning embers before entering the door. Which is your first test. If you win, you will see flying mountains before you which will make you reach the volcano. All these mountains are connected by invisible stairs which you need to find and climb yourself. This is a strange labyrinth made of mountains and stairs, you can reach there only by crossing it. One last thing, don't stay on any mountain beyond a few moments otherwise it will fall with your weight and death is certain. Also, if you do not cross it before sunset, you will be imprisoned in it forever and will never be able to come back."

"I have no information beyond this for your", the Hunter said.

"That will be enough for me! Let's go now", Samuel replied.

Samuels met everyone. He got ready for his onward journey and went to meet Purva before leaving. She was much better now but her wound was not completely healed. She held Samuel's hand and said softly in his ear, "Where would I go without you, we are together for a lifetime. Be it happiness, sorrow, or any struggle. I never expressed myself till my last breath I am only yours". Samuel kissed her forehead and said, "Me too".

He left for the deciding stage of his journey. Purva's words resonated within him. He was very happy, confident as never before, and had new positive energy. This is what is the power of love, though she was not with him, they were together as his motivation.

Samuel had reached the exit door. It was a huge door made of stone with a sand lock. The hunter rubbed his hand and unlocked the door. The door began to open slowly, and a burning ember was before him. The fire was so dense that anything could be burned to ashes in seconds. But Samuel didn't care. He moved forward with determination. His feet were getting blisters, but he kept moving.

The brain is the most powerful in the human body. If one can keep aligned is well, keeps a tough control and sharp focus, every trouble gets easy, and each closed door gets open automatically. Samuel did the same, he had aligned himself as well nothing could distract him now. In no time he crossed the door.

A beautiful scene of blue sky with numerous flying mountains was before him. Some were lush green, some made of hard rock. Some were small and many were extra-large in size.

All the mountains were at a great distance from each other and were slowly changing their positions. There was a deep ditch at the bottom. Beautiful birds were flying and chirping. The thing to note was that those birds used to sit in between the gap of the mountains but were not falling. Samuel understood that wherever birds are sitting are surely the invisible stairs connecting the mountains, but he was also cautious about not falling into any trap and maintaining a good speed.

Samuel firmly held the hammer given by The Hunter and stepped forward. He decided that he would cross the entire path, taking only small mountains. He jumped on the first mountain while running and no birds were sitting in between. He quickly struck all the corners of the mountain gently with the hammer and heard a sound clinking sound 'Tak...Tanak...Tak'; the invisible stairs instantly appeared before him. He followed the pattern and started to cross in speed. Wherever the birds were sitting he followed the path and were not he found the stairs by hitting on the mountain corners.

Now he had come to the last mountain which is in much isolation. There were no birds around hence no hint for the stairs further. He started hitting all the corners of the mountain but neither any voice came, nor any stairs appeared before him.

"There has to be away," he said to himself. He was keeping a watch on the sunset and realized that less time was left.

He fired arrows from his bow in all four directions, but nothing happened. He looked around curiously. Then he realized that the mountain was getting surrounded by thick clouds. All the clouds were white but the color of one cloud in the middle at much height was constantly changing. He flooded the bow and struck the cloud. As soon as the arrow hit, a long thick rope started hanging. Also, in the middle of the clouds, a circular path was formed.

Samuel understood the way forward before him, which has to be crossed by this rope. But that rope was at some distance from the mountain. He took a few steps back and, running fast, jumped towards the rope, and entered the path built between the clouds.

Samuel began to fall quickly, then a huge peacock caught him and dropped him to the ground.

And this is it, Samuel was in crystal valley.

All around it was crystals of different types, sizes, and shapes. As the rays of the sun were falling on them, golden light was spreading all around. A beautiful rainbow was also formed on one side of the sky. His eyes fell on a corner of the valley, where a thick torrent of magma from the mountain above was falling on the crystals. There was a lot of smoke in that place, all the crystals were dark red.

A huge pair of peacocks was continuously eating the magma falling on them. Samuels was watching in amazement, how they were eating the magma so comfortably without getting hurt. He kept watching carefully. They were continuously clearing those crystals so that the rays of the sun kept falling on him properly. As the rays fell, a thick golden line formed in the middle of each crystal making them sharper. From the far distance, we appeared like crystal arrows.

Believing this is what he was here for, Samuel moved ahead and as he approached. A peacock turned toward him and warned him in a threatening tone, "Stop there and don't dare to move forward."

Samuel took out his sword to defend himself and said, "Who are you to stop me?"

"Put this sword back in its sheath and bring a humility in your voice, kid, lest I burn you to ashes", Peacock said.

"Maybe you don't know, who I am. One blow of my sward will break you into pieces", said Samuel with a warning.

Peacock smiled and turned towards him saying "Oh! That's amazing I would like to know you then." In the blink of an eye, his body became like a human, but his neck was that of a peacock.

He stood in front of Samuel and challenged him.

Samuel struck him with the sword, and as soon as the sword touched the peacock, the sword melted and fell.

"This was contrary to his imagination", Samuel looked at him in wonder and asked, "Who are you?".

"I am Milind, the Peacock king and this valley are under my protection. It has the most valuable and dangerous metals, stones, and crystals. My responsibility is to ensure that only deserving and needy people are only able to get benefited here. No greedy, deceitful and evil person has any right over this valley and its treasures."

"You are a good, brave, and kind-hearted person, only then you could have reached here. But I cannot allow you to take anything from here without knowing the purpose of your coming here. Tell your target, if it is according to the rules here, then you can take whatever you want from here."

Introducing himself, Samuel told him his full story and his goal.

Milind was lost in deep worry after listening to him.

"Am I allowed to take what I want from here?", Samuel asked requesting.

"Definitely", he replied.

He placed a sharp, long, and strong crystal in Samuel's hand. This was the same dark red colour crystal with a thick golden line in the middle.

"This is what you need to hit your target", he said, "But..."

"But what?", Samuel asked.

"Your target is such that you will need it at the right time, in perfect shape, and condition. Even if you take it from here now, I am sure this would solve your purpose". Milind explained.

"So, what should I be doing now, I can't bring my target here? And by saying this, don't you think my purpose of being here and completely defeated", Samuel replied with many worries.

"A sincere effort made ever never gets defeated. Surely, your target can't be here, but this crystal can reach you when you need it at the right time", Milind said.

"But how this will happen", Samuel asked, surprised.

Milind picked up the ashes of the magma, folded in a piece of cloth and something in Samuel's ear while placing it in his hand.

Samuel shook his head in consent. Milind had told him the way the arrow will reach him at the right time and how to use it.

"Now you should go back soon. Many people are waiting for you for justice of all the injustice and atrocities done to them", Milind said to Samuel.

Milind gave a sward to him saying, "You would need this in your war."

A peacock landed before him.

"He will take you back", Milind said.

Samuel seeks his blessings, boarded the peacock, and flew back.

Soon he reached the desert and came to Hunter's hut where everyone was waiting for him. Leaving him there, the peacock flew back.

Flutus came running and hugged him. He was delighted to see him back.

"Captain Mojo salutes you for your bravery and the great person you are", he said with teary eyes.

Purva could not hold back her tears of happiness anymore. She hugged Samuel tightly and kissed his lips. "Welcome back my prince", she said crying.

"I knew you'd succeed", Hunter said.

Samuel put his hand on her shoulder and said, "I can't even thank you enough for your help."

"Can I request one more favor?", Samuel asked humbly.

"Sure, tell me what I can do", Hunter replied.

Samuel told him about Dikaso and what all happened while they were crossing the sea.

"Can you ask your dwarf to treat him as well?", Samuel requested.

He agreed and asked one of them to go with him for treating Dikaso.

They all thanked Hunter and said goodbye.

For their return, the Hunter opened the door to Dessert, and soon they came to the seashore.

Flutus takes out the small ship from his bag and placed it in the water and it became as big as before.

All the people boarded it and started their return journey.

They had come a long way and were near the hill where Dikaso used to live.

Samuel asked Captain Mojo to stop the ship and boarding the Thunder along with the dwarf man flew towards the hill.

They soon landed there, "Who is that?", Dikaso asked in a painful voice.

"It's me, Samuel, how are you feeling now?", he asked.

Dikaso did not reply to anything but rather asked, "Who is it with you?"

"Oh, he is a very gentle cute little man, I have come with him so that your wound can be healed."

"That's next to impossible", said Dikaso with a sad heart. "Now I am just waiting for my end."

"Don't say that I will fix you and anyway I need your help too", said Samuel.

"I am no longer of any use to you. And as far as helping you is concerned, what can I do because I owe you that you left me alive and tried to stop the flow of blood from my eyes, due to which I and our species are still alive."

Samuel told the Dwarf Man to heal Dikaso. He broke a long hair from his beard and sealed both his eyes with a protruding object. And then he rubbed his spit on both his wounds. As soon as he did this, both his eyes stopped bleeding completely.

"You are perfectly fine now, and nothing will happen to you and your species", Samuel said happily.

Dikaso was glad and his happiness knew no bounds. "I will never forget this favor of yours", he said.

"You are my friend and it's no favor to you. Friends only help each other", Samuel consoled him and spoke.

"How can I help you, my friend?", Dikaso asked.

Samuel told him about the decisive battle of his life and asked him for the help of his army.

Dikaso happily agreed and said giving him a flute, "Whenever you need me and my army, face the sky and shed it loudly. We will all reach out to your aid immediately."

Samuel thanked him and headed back to the ship.

Chapter 8: The Conclusion

After a long struggle, one day the detectives of Haliba got the news of 'Lipika'.

On receiving the news, he immediately reached the monastery and ordered his soldiers to take Lipika captive..

As they entered the monastery, shocked to see someone there.

It was **'Lionel'**, meditating under a tree. Lionel's father was a trusted advisor and political mentor to King Virat.'

Lionel, Nirvana, and Markooz were childhood friends. Lionel was inclined towards Markooz from the beginning but when he came to know about his wrong deeds and the truth about him, he started to distance himself from him.

When King Virat came to know about Amara's truth, it was Lionel's father who suggested severe punishment for Markooz and his mother according to political norms.

As time progressed and Markooz became powerful, he formed his army and made a plan to take his revenge by destroying Thanjavur.

He knew very well that this would not be possible till Nirvana was alive. He needed a highly skilled and powerful warrior to fight by his side and lead his army.

And that warrior was 'Lionel' who was not only powerful but one of the most skilled in war strategy.

Markooz requested Lionel to help him in the war, explaining their friendship and the tyranny he had suffered. But Lionel did not agree and decided to support Nirvana.

One day Lionel was returning from the palace with his father when Markooz came to meet him again and asked for his help in the war. Seeing Markooz, Lionel's father uttered abusive words to him, in anger he attacked and killed him.

Lionel attacked Markooz. But now he was also very powerful and had deadly magical powers. He badly wounded Lionel but did not kill him. He left him alive and started leaving.

Lionel told him that he would support Thanjavur and Nirvana till his last breath and cursed him that it would have a very painful end. On hearing this, Markooz's anger knew no bounds and he ordered the spirits to attack him. Spirits inflicted many internal wounds on his body. While leaving he said, you will live for sure but will never be able to fight again. I want you alive to see the rise of Markooz and the end of Thanjavur and Nirvana.

Today, Haliba had a very good chance to become a hero in front of Markooz by taking both Lipika and Lionel captive.

He entered the ashram with his soldiers. Lipika saw Haliba and his men marching towards Lionel, she attacked them for his protection. There was fierce archery from both sides. Lipika was a very skilled warrior and Haliba and his soldiers had to run for their lives.

Lipika turned towards Lionel, she saw that many arrows had pierced his body, and he was taking his last breath. Hearing the noise, Durgashakti and all the people of the ashram came running. There was a lot of blood oozing from his body, and he died.

Samuel, Purva, and Flutus had also returned and were on their way to the ashram.

Prakus, Durgashakti, Lipika and others, paid tribute to Lionel.

Slowly and with small steps, Fiona came out of her hut and, keeping a state posture on Lionel's body, said "Me, my family & my people will always be grateful to you, you have performed your duty with true devotion."

By that time, Samuel had also reached there. He learned about the death of the incident at the ashram.

Lionel was cremated by Samael with all due respect.

"In this burning pyre of Lionel, Markooz and his empire will also have to be consumed,

With Lionel's sacrifice, Markooz's end begins,

With Lionel's pyre today, we all must light a victory torch in our hearts,

This torch should be lit with the end of our enemy.

Are you all ready to join me in this decisive battle?

Are you all dressed up!", Samuel sighed.

Everyone replied in a zealous voice, "Yes! we are ready."

The same day evening, Parkus, Durgashakti, Lipka, Purva, Flutus, and important soldiers of Parkus's army gathered in the main hall of the ashram.

"How many soldiers do we have and what is their specialty?",
Samuel asked Parkus.

"About five thousand, about eight hundred are excellent
archers whose aim is perfect. About fifteen hundred are
skilled swordsmen and the rest are skilled in other battles.
There is so much courage and confidence in our army that it
will outweigh the army of millions", Parkus replied.

Samuel pointed to Purva and she placed a very map in front
of everyone. Everyone started looking at it carefully.

"What's the plan?", Parkus asked Samuel.

"Thanjavur", this fight is between Thanjavur and Markooz
and it must re-exist. The end of 'Mazar' will mark the sunrise
of Thanjavur and the beginning of the end of Markooz."

"Presently, it is under the control of 'Zian'. Our victory will
begin with his death and his capturing 'Thanjavur' back. That
will be our biggest attack on Markooz."

"Spread the news among the people by your spies that
'Samuel', the son of Nirvana, is coming to an end Markooz.
Queen Fiona and Durgashakti are also alive. Also, send a
message to Zian that if he wants the safety of his life, it is
advisable for him to run away otherwise his death is certain. I
believe that even after so many years, we still have many
trusted people there who are waiting for justice. Everyone,
there is troubled by the atrocities of him and his son. This
news will cause rebellion among the people, and they will
support us", Samuel said to Parkus.

Samuel garlands Parkus with a magic garland of Kalazi and
appoints him a commander and asks him to lead the army.

He urged his mother 'Durgashakti' to leave for 'Phalsa' and reach Thanjavur at the earliest with all his supporters, army, and as many as deadly weapons. He ordered Purva and Captain Mojo to go with her.

"We will attack the Mazar tomorrow morning itself", Samuel said.

He requested Parkus to accompany him with his trusted soldiers, all the archers, and two hundred swordsmen and asked him to send the rest soldiers under the supervision of Flutus and wait for further instructions.

"Zain has deadly bodyguards and a huge army. It might be difficult with just a small number of soldiers. Ideally, we should go in full force", Parkus said.

"You are right, but I believe we always take up two kinds of fights to defeat an enemy, one on the battlefield or the other mentally. Victory in war does not depend on the number of soldiers and warriors one has, but on the right strategy, fighting skills, and unwavering confidence. Markooz and his son Zain are proud of their military power and magical powers with a firm belief that no one can defeat them. I want to first hit on their confidence & break it. They have spread the hollow fear of his power by oppressing everyone to date. He shows the whole world that he is very powerful and invincible. He has created a web of fear and confusion all around him, and the victims are the people of his kingdom, his army, and everyone who is with him either out of choice or fear. Everyone has accepted his fears and atrocities as their destiny because they think that Markooz will never end and even if it can happen, they are not capable of it. Everyone accepted to live in darkness to survive. We have to give a new light of hope to the world and all the people by taking them out of fear. And when this happens, he will find himself standing alone. Tomorrow's day is very important; I will kill Zain alone. All you have to do is, remove the obstacle for me to reach him. Tomorrow, with the end of Zain, we will get the support of every person who is tired of tolerating this arrogance and tyranny. Tomorrow we will get the support of a huge masses and there will be rebellion in all its states. That would be Markooz's biggest defeat, and his pride would be shattered", Samuel said.

"I have no hesitation in saying that you think like your father, and are equally wise and brave like him", said Parkus.

As planned, Samuel's warning of war had reached Zain. He was trembling with anger and was ready for battle.

The next day both the armies were faces to face. Zain had built a maze of warriors around him, which was not easy to break.

On the Zain's side, there were innumerable soldiers, demons, and great weapons of the deadly attack. Zain was riding on a very big elephant surrounded by his bodyguards.

On the other side, Samuel was riding on his horse 'Thunder', accompanied by Parkus and a small army bay. Seeing this, Zain's general 'Kazashi' laughed very loudly and said warning Samuel, "If the hobby of suicide has been fulfilled, then you should go back my child, my Great King Zain will let you go otherwise we will not ever leave your bones", and laughed out loud. Seeing this Jain and all his warriors and soldiers also started laughing out loud. The battlefield resonated with their laughter.

Samuel shot an arrow into his bow and struck Kazashi. His arrow pierced his forehead and he fell to the ground.

Now it was a deep silent battlefield and only the loud sound of the feet of Samuel's horse. He was rapidly moving towards Zain and his army. No warrior had any answer for his attack. His arrows kept penetrating the enemies. No one could stand in front of him, whether a warrior or a devil. In no time, he destroyed more than half of the Zain's army. His speed was such that he had left Parkus and his army far behind. Zain's army started fleeing. Samuel broke through every maze and reached Zain.

Zain was very nervous. The fear of death was visible on his face. He never imagined that this would happen. Only one warrior had destroyed it all.

His bodyguards surrounded Samuel from all sides and attacked him. Samuel dropped his bow and took up the sword. It was the same sword that was given to him by Milind in Crystal Valley. He slashed every weapon raised towards him, and as soon as his sword touched the bodyguards, they were reduced to ashes. He killed everyone.

Zain was trembling with fear and fell from his elephant. Gathering courage, he attacked Samuel, but in a jiffy, Samuel severed his neck from the torso.

Samuel had won the battle. He rode on his horse and marched towards the city. Arriving at the city gate, he broke the placard written 'Mazar' with his arrow and waved the flag to Thanjavur. The soldiers opened the city gates for him. He proceeded to the palace with Parkus and his army.

As he went ahead, tears started flowing from his eyes. He had come back to his kingdom, his home after a long time which he had to leave a night. The memories of his childhood started revolving around him.

All the people and soldiers of the city were standing on either side of the road and were looking at him with wet eyes. There was satisfaction and hope in their eyes.

Samuel whispered in Parkus's ear, "Tell your army to take all the main gates of the city and the palace in your continuum."

He went ahead and started entering the palace. He was emotional and content but knew that the storm was yet to come. His victory over Thanjavur was the first step to his success. He hoisted the ancient flag of Thanjavur on the palace and declared his victory.

He was also aware that not all the people were in his favor, and he organized a public meeting to avoid the state rebellion. More people came there than he expected.

Samuel addressed the gathering, "This vast kingdom was a symbol of its integrity centuries ago. To make it great and happy, my grandfather Ratan Singh made every effort and gave a contented, and secure life to his citizens. Under his leadership, it became a powerful and prosperous state which selflessly served all the people.

His son, King Virat, while performing his duties, made this kingdom more prosperous and prouder. But the nefarious intentions, greed, hatred, and lust of his descendant Markooz pushed this state into such darkness that it is not possible to emerge. My father Nirvana performed his duty and sacrificed himself.

I do not know who all of you are and how many descendants are from this, but I know very well that all of you are oppressed by his tyranny. I have decided that I will free this world from the tyranny of Markooz and today is the beginning of this end.

Me and many people with me have come back to their homes today. As much as this state is mine, it belongs to all of you too. I don't know from where and under what circumstances you people came here. Perhaps some of you will have descendants from here. All of you can live here as before, but now no one will be oppressed and I will try my best to live a happy life for all of you. But the one who does not agree with me can leave this kingdom immediately. If anyone is found to be revolting, the only result will be the death penalty."

There was an eerie silence, everyone whispering amongst themselves. Tearing silence, all the people shouted about the greatness of Samuel and announced, "We are with you!"

Samuel got the support of all the masses.

On the other hand, Markooz received the news of the murder of his son Zain. Haliba reached with some soldiers with his dead body.

"Who is he?", Markooz asked.

Haliba replied nervously, "His name is Samuel, and described himself as the son of Nirvana. He single-handedly destroyed our entire army and killed our beloved Prince Zain."

"He is a deadlier and much more efficient warrior as like Nirvana", said Haliba.

Hearing this, Markooz lost his cool and tattled Haliba's neck with his knife angrily saying, "Did I ask? Did I ask? Did I even ask?"

Haliba fell to the ground and died.

Markooz picked up Zain's dead body and left his palace. He reached the same cave where he had created & imprisoned an army of innumerable souls with his magical powers.

But there, he had imprisoned someone else as well, the severed head of his father 'Virat'.

The evening when Markooz's mother Amra died, he went to the palace. His anger and hatred were so fierce that he killed his father and brought his severed head with him. He kept him alive and used to visit him often.

Today, he came with the dead body of his son, Zain.

"Can you hear me father", he called out to Virat.

"Today is a very happy day for you, because Samuel, the son of your good son The Great Nirvana, killed Zain, the son of your evil son, that's me. Good thing, after all, you got one good news in all these years", Markooz said.

"Both my sons were good; the only difference is that you chose the path of evil and followed it and your brother Nirvana did all good and performed all his duties. No matter how great & powerful the evil, it always has an end. For all these years, I tried to convince you to come back to the right path, but your ambitions made you even more cruel and despicable. And as far as I am concerned, I am a tree whose own branches have cut it down and destroyed it. This is not only the beginning of your end but the end of an era in which people only got pain, tyranny, and tragedy and their life was no less than a curse."

"But we both are responsible for this. My ambition in good faith gave birth to this whole incident. But a lie and your ambition, jealousy, and the desire for revenge destroyed everything. At the time of Amra's death, you had the opportunity to make the right choice, but you chose the wrong path as your mother did. Which became a punishment for a kingdom, its people, and a family. You were glad that you destroyed everything. But wasn't your kingdom too? Didn't you kill own your brother? But forget it, you killed your father too and made him stay alive just to prove yourself."

"Having power is important and necessary too, but most important is channelize it well for the good. This is what is the difference between a 'Human' and a 'Demon'. No one becomes a Human or a Demon by birth and powers. Our actions & choice make us who we want to be. "

"I loved & trusted your mother immensely. And it doesn't matter to me whether she was a human or a demon because when we love someone, be it good or flaws are all ours. But she cheated, lied, and kept me in the dark. Not only this, but she has also veiled your deeds and reality, the result of which is this horrific destruction. If this had not happened, everyone would have been together and happy. You are my son, and I am sad for you too. But you have shed the blood of countless innocents and your death will be your atonement. You have to pay for your every sin with every drop of your blood. I wish

I had come to know in time, and I would have done something for you", said Virat.

"I wish I could do something, huh....I did not come here to listen to your speech by dearest father but rather to tell you that I am going to destroy your kingdom and people once again. Last time some people survived, my mistake, now it will not happen. Now there will be annihilation, such a war that even the soul of the one who sees it will tremble", Markooz went on speaking in anger and broke all the glass bottles kept in his cave and opened the wooden boxes in which the army made of deadly spirits was imprisoned.

He had set out towards his decisive battle. The words of his father were echoing in his mind and were shaking his heart. He realized what his father said was right, but the jealousy, anger, ego, and power had gone to his head so much that even today it was difficult for him to differentiate between wrong and right.

Samuel was preparing for the next battle. Durgshakti had reached Thanjavur with soldiers and weapons. With him was the return of many people who had to migrate from here many years ago.

In the kingdoms that were not under Markooz's control, Samuel invited all of them to join him in the war, but because of Mark's fear, no one came along.

And the crucial day had come.

The huge army of Markooz surrounded Thanjavur from all sides. The two armies were facing each other. This was the same ground where the battle of Nirvana and Markooz took place years ago.

Samuel's army was like a drop of the ocean before Markooz's vast army, but his warriors were full of confidence.

Markooz's new general, Dulter, jokingly ordered his army, "Go ahead and crush these ants, I don't want to be late for evening victory".

A detachment full of soldiers and demons attacked.

Samuel, Purva, Parkus, and all the other archers rained arrows on them. Their attack was beyond Dulter's thinking, seeing that his army's corpses began to pile up. On the other hand, Flutus was killing all the demons with his magical powers.

Dulter himself moved forward and the situation began to change. The rain of arrows did not affect him. He was a skilled and dangerous warrior. Prakus turned to him and both of them started fighting.

Now, a large detachment of Markooz's army had attacked, and the situation was not in Samuel's favor. He called for Dikaso and his Crocodile army by playing the flute. Within moments they reached and attacked the enemies and began to destroy them rapidly.

It was becoming difficult for Parkus to control Dulter. He was very injured and was struggling continuously. He could not last long and Dulter killed him by slitting his throat.

Dulter went ahead and launched a deadly attack on the Crocodile army and went on killing it.

There was chaos in the army. All the soldiers got frightened by the death of their commander Parkus and started running for their lives. Seeing this, Dulter started laughing out loud.

While stopping his soldiers Samuel said, "Have you been struggling for so many years to escape from the battlefield today?"

"In front of you is the enemy who killed your loved ones and made you homeless, isn't your blood boiling?"

"If we don't stop them today, they will again enter our houses and rape your mother and sisters. Is your blood not boiling thinking of this? He killed your teacher and commander; he is now laughing aloud. Isn't blood boiling even after seeing this? But my blood is boiling. I am going to clear my motherland from these wicked people. I am going for every person who believed in me. I am going to avenge the death of each of my companions. I am going for the end of this tarnished era and the beginning of a new era where there will be happiness, prosperity, and happiness."

"If any one of you has a little courage left and wants to come with me, then pick up your sword, your bow. But remember, with just one blow, the neck of the enemy will have to be separated from the body. Let's register ourselves in history to be remembered as a warrior who beheaded all his enemies."

Samuel rode on his horse Thunder and attacked the enemy.

He moved towards Daulter, before he could understand anything, Samuel struck with his sword, and he and his horse were cut in two. He took out the divine garland of Kalari from Prakus's neck and wore it so that the army of souls could not harm him.

The speed of thunder and the unmistakable and deadly blow of Samuel had struck the battlefield like a storm, and everyone was falling like dry leaves. The dead bodies fell on the ground, but their heads were cut off. There were bodies of warriors on the running horses, but their heads had been cut off.

Behind him, Purva and queen Lipika was also killing the enemies. On seeing Queen Lipika, the invincible army of Kuntal gave up arms in her honor and started leaving the battlefield.

He kept going inside Markooz's army, destroying the enemy. He was alone but no warrior on that side could stop Samuel today.

An arrow came flying and struck Samuel's chest. Flying from the horse, he fell to the ground. He got up and pulled the arrow out of his chest. Then another arrow came and hit the other side of his chest.

Markooz had arrived on the battlefield. Perhaps there was only one who could compete with Samuel. Seeing him, Samuel's eyes began to burn with anger. He also threw the second arrow out of his body and got back on his horse. His wound was bleeding, but he didn't care. Nor did he feel pain.

Both were face to face.

He was riding his four-headed horse in a black dress. In his hand was a long, strong sword. Sunset was about to set and as the sun was setting his big red eyes looked even more frightening and scary. Now no soldier or warrior was fighting. All eyes were on both of them. The people of Thanjavur started gathering around the battlefield. No one wanted to miss watching this decisive battle.

"Haliba had said, you are a better warrior than Nirvana, but you fell from my single blow. You have disappointed me a lot, poor he unnecessarily lost his life praising you", said Markooz.

"Perhaps this was the battlefield and the same place where you are standing was the dead body of your father. Your father faced me with great courage but poor him, he sacrificed his life to save his people. He was a fool, if he had fought with his army, he might have lived a few more days."

"You too came to fight alone with me like your idiot father and on the top, you believe that you would be able to kill 'The Great Markzoo." Funny!!!

Growling he said, "I am darkness and I have no end. Whoever tries to come near me, I swallow him."

"I didn't have to be here to kill you, but I didn't want to lose the fun of watching you die. Oh...God thank you so very much that you gave me the opportunity to kill Samuel too like his father", Markooz laughed.

I drank only the blood of your father's chest, but I will cut you into such small pieces that your mother will get tired of joining them together. Markooz said with a warning.

"No matter how dark the darkness may be, a spark of light becomes a torch and illuminates everything. Your end is here and will be today only. This is your last night because tomorrow will be your end with a new sunrise."

"My father, while performing the duty of a true king, ensured the safety of his people. He was true and brave, he stood alone on this battlefield to fight with you. He not only destroyed your entire army but also left you half dead."

"He was not a cheater like you. You killed him by deceit. But I have the answer to your every deception and black magic", Samuel said.

Hearing this, Markooz was furious and struck Samuel with his magic power. Samuel defended himself by holding out his sword.

He called upon his army of deadly spirits and instructed them to attack Samuel, but because of the divine rosary around his neck, they could not harm him.

They attacked each other and a fierce battle started. The spark of their sword quarrel was so strong that it could burn anyone with ashes. There was a tussle between both of them and both were badly affected. Fighting night had passed and the morning was about to come.

Milind's words were in Samuel's mind and the time had come for what he said.

While he was leaving Crystal Island, Milind said in his ear while giving him Lava's ashes.

"The best time to strike your enemy would be at sunrise. The sunrise rays are most powerful and pure. When the sun's rays will fall on these crystals and heat the lava inside them, its strike would be deadly and infallible. Whenever you will be in the need of crystal arrows, I will ensure to send the best & fresh lava-filled crystals to you.

Milind had said, rub the ashes of the lava on your bow. By doing this, the arrow of the crystal will appear. Its attack will be impenetrable, so attack your enemy with full strength, faith and dedication. But remember, only five arrows can come to you.

Now, the war was nearing its end. Samuel rubbed lave ashes on his bow and immediately a very sharp and long crystal arrow appeared. Inside it was filled with lava spewing fire. With the first ray of the sun, Samuel shot his first arrow at Markooz. The arrow went out penetrating through his body. The blow was so fatal that he fell from his horse and started moaning in pain.

Samuel knew that Markooz's life was in his horse. He hit the horse with another arrow and he fell crying.

Markooz and his horse were both badly injured. Blood was flowing and their bodies were burning with the heat of the lava. But both were alive. Samuel changed direction and fired the third arrow in such a way that it passed through, piecing together Markooz and his horse. Both the wounded were lying on the ground, bleeding profusely but they were still alive.

Markooz's moaning with pain had now turned into his laughter. He laughed and said, "Half-truths are of no use, only Markooz knows the secret and truth behind his death". You can injure me, but you cannot kill me nor my horse. we will live even if our bodies are torn into pieces.

Markooz was lying wounded on the ground, laughing loudly.

Samuel now aimed and struck Markooz's chest with the fourth arrow. The arrow hit his chest, and his right arm was cut off by its explosion. But he still kept on laughing and said, 'My death is impossible, little boy'.

Now Samuel was worried because now he was left only with "The Last Crystal Arrow" and it was his last chance.

He invoked the fifth arrow and aimed at the horse. Lipika had told him that Markooz has hidden his heart in his horse and as long as it beats neither of them can die.

There was a lot of noise on the battlefield, but only silence in Samuel's ears. Pointed an arrow at the horse's chest aiming at his heart. His hands were trembling, and his mind was disturbed.

Maybe he was not sure. He kept changing the positions and was yet to release the final arrow.

While he kept shifting his aim at the horse's body, he noticed that every time he pointed towards the neck, a dot appears which was not in the case of his chest or the head.

Maybe this was the right sign for him. He decided that he would hit the horse's neck. But he was still confused.

His eyes turned to Purva.

Purva looked at him with confidence and with the gesture of her eyes, she asked him to shoot the arrow.

Samuel adjusted himself in such a direction that his arrows could pierce all the four necks of the horse at once.

Seeing this, Markooz panicked and ran towards Samuel shouting to stop him. But by then he had shot the arrow.

He shot arrows with all his might; His arrow pierced all the four necks of the horse at once. As soon as the arrow hit, the horse started tormented with pain. Now the end of both was near and they started breathing their last.

Markooz grabbed Samuel's neck tightly and with his sharp nails made deep wounds and bruises on his neck and chest. The celestial garland around Samuel's neck was broken, the glass vial in it also broken and the fluid-filled in it spread all over his wounds and got absorbed in it.

Markooz's grip weakened, and he took his last breath, saying, "Every sunrise also has a sunset". After which darkness swallows the light. I am darkness; I can be eradicated but my end is impossible. I will come back "again!".

The sun was shining in the sky and Markooz had come to his end. With his last breath, his magical world began to be destroyed. There was a huge explosion in the cave which destroyed all the wooden boxes and glass bottles kept. Eventually, King Virat also got liberation. Thousands of dead bodies of his army disappeared from the battlefield.

The next morning, holding Samuel's hand, with small and slow steps, Queen Fiona entered the palace. Durgashakti, Purva, Lipika, Flutus, and others were also with her. It was a very emotional moment for all of them. They all had very golden memories of this palace, but much had been destroyed. There was satisfaction on their faces for their new beginning. With teary eyes, they paid homage to King Virat, Nirvana, and every warrior who died in this struggle.

Flutus was made the king of Kuntal and he decided to rule under the protection of Thanjavur.

Samuel was made the king of Thanjavur and married Purva.

After a year they were blessed with a baby boy whom he named 'Anagha'

Five years had passed, one day Anagha was playing in the courtyard of the palace. Then a white dove fell in front of him from the sky. She was groaning in pain.

He was attracted to her and he picked her up. After a while, the dove died. Anagha thought that he had fallen asleep in his hand and tried to wake her up. When the maid standing nearby saw this, she took the dove from Anagha's hand and kept it under a tree.

She picked up Anagha in her lap and took him inside, but he kept looking at the dove. Samuel was watching all this from afar.

That same evening, Purva and Samuel were in their room when Anagha came running. He was carrying the same white dove which was dead but now she was alive.

He pointed innocuously toward Samuel, saying, "Dad, I've brought this dead dove back to life. It will die in broad daylight, but it will come back to life when it gets dark. How good magic is that? Can I play with her?"

Samuel kept looking at Anagha in shock & surprise.

Was it the return of Markooz?!

You can know more about Ravi Sharma by emailing him at ravi.connectme@gmail.com

Printed by Libri Plureos GmbH in Hamburg,
Germany